THE SUICIDE SQUAD:
WANTED—IN THREE PINE COFFINS
AND OTHER STORIES

ACE G·MAN

WANTED—IN THREE PINE COFFINS

AND OTHER STORIES

By Emile C. Tepperman

POPULAR PUBLICATIONS • 2022

PUBLISHING HISTORY

"Wanted—In Three Pine Coffins" originally appeared in the September 1941 (Vol. 8, No. 4) issue of *Ace G-Man Stories* magazine. "The Suicide Squad's Private War" originally appeared in the December 1941 (Vol. 9, No. 1) issue of *Ace G-Man Stories* magazine. "—For Tomorrow We Die!" originally appeared in the February 1942 (Vol. 9, No. 2) issue of *Ace G-Man Stories* magazine. Copyright 2022 by Argosy Communications, Inc. All rights reserved.

WANTED—
IN THREE PINE COFFINS

CHAPTER 1
THE REAPER STALKS

A MAN named Petrie, unaware that he had only one more day of life credited to him, glanced swiftly about, then stepped into a telegraph office. He went to one of the desks and seated himself in such a way that he could look through the plate glass window out at the street.

His hand was steady as he took one of the blanks and printed his message in block letters:

> MR. JASON WELLINGTON
> HOTEL HALSEY
> WASHINGTON, D.C.
> AUNT MINNIE BUNKO IN PLACTIC VERDANT
> TONIGHT. GRISLY LATE HORN OF GAMMA BUT
> NORING FITTEN ZENEDU. CRAM FOURTEEN
> THROUGH THE MIDDLE.
> PETRIE

As he wrote he consulted a small card, which he held under the light in a certain way. When he was through, he took out a match, lit it, and burned the card down to the last corner, holding it between thumb and forefinger until it was nothing but ash.

2

Hot flame seared their faces, and bullets whipped a leaden hail about them.

Still watching the street carefully, he took his block-lettered message to the counter, and handed the form to the girl.

She frowned. "Sorry, but we don't accept code messages, except for the Army or Navy—"

She broke off at sight of the identification card case which the man, Petrie, opened and flashed before her.

"Oh, of course, Lieutenant," the girl said quickly, "This message will go out at once!"

"I'll wait to make sure," said Petrie, quietly.

He turned his back to the counter, and continued to stare outside. His ear followed the clicking of the key which sent his message. Apparently he was an expert in Morse Code, for he nodded when the operator had finished. He must have had that message of his memorized letter perfect.

He said, "That was correct. Now, if anyone should come in and make inquiries as to what message I sent—"

The girl nodded. "I understand, Lieutenant. You can be sure I won't say anything."

Petrie smiled crookedly. "I have no choice but to trust you. I hope—for the sake of all of us—that I haven't made a mistake."

He turned and went out, walking warily, still unaware that his credit account in the book of life was running down to the narrow margin of twenty-three hours. Perhaps he didn't care.

The electric clock in the telegraph office said: *Four-fifty-one....*

JASON WELLINGTON hurried out of the Hotel Halsey in Washington, D.C. and rushed to a cab.

"War Department!" he ordered. "As fast as you can!"

4

Five minutes later, the man named Jason Wellington was standing, breathless, at a desk in an office on the fourth floor of the War Department. Behind the desk sat a gray-haired man in civilian dress. He held the rank of Major-General, and he was in command of every ramified branch of the United States Military Intelligence.

Jason Wellington thrust a telegraph blank into the general's hand.

"This just came, sir. God, we've got to move fast! Petrie couldn't telephone, because my wire was tapped, and I had inserted the coded warning advertisement in the personal columns of all the newspapers where our men are operating. There may still be time—"

The general's eyes dropped to the telegram. Underneath the printed capital letters, Wellington had written the decoded message:

> GESTAPO AGENTS HERE IN FORCE PLOT-TING SOMETHING BIG FOR TOMORROW NIGHT. SUPREME CHIEF OF NAZI AGENTS OPERATING FROM THIS CITY. THEY HAVE SPOTTED ME AND I AM HELPLESS. NEED AID. SEND HELP CORNER OF SEVENTH AND MYRTLE TOMORROW AT THREE-THIRTY USE IDENTIFICATION CODE FOURTEEN.

The general's face was grim. "Aunt Minnie," he said.

Aunt Minnie was one of the half-dozen code words which Military Intelligence used to designate the German Secret Service in America. Each of the code words referred to a different, specific branch of those activities. "Aunt Minnie" meant that branch which was being operated through the consular offices, directed by agents who enjoyed diplomatic immunity and who could move with much greater freedom than ordinary agents.

"If Aunt Minnie is involved, we've got to watch our step," the general said. "I have orders not to do anything which might provoke a diplomatic break at this time. Have you any men in the Coast City area whom you could send in there?"

Wellington shook his head. "This isn't a job for Military Intelligence any longer, sir. Any action taken by a United States Army officer would take official color—"

"Yes, yes," the general interrupted. "Yet, we've got to get help to Petrie!"

"But how, sir? Even if we could send our own men in there, we haven't got a sufficient number to be of any help. If Aunt Minnie is operating in force, as Petrie says, we should give him a couple of dozen men. The most we could spare from other duties on the coast would be five or six."

"I have another idea," said the general. "Leave it to me." FIVE MINUTES after Jason Wellington had gone, the general got out of a staff car in front of the Department of Justice Building on Constitution Avenue. Three minutes later, he was talking with the Chief of the Federal Bureau of Investigation, in a room where no one could possibly overhear a word of their conversation.

"Have you got two dozen men on the coast, whom you could assign to a dangerous, critical mission?" he asked.

"Sorry," said the Chief. "The answer's no, General. We're

6

increasing the F.B.I. staff as fast as possible, but we're still short of men—"

"You've got to help me," interrupted the general. "You've *got* to find the men." He produced the decoded telegram. "It's a job for a squad of men who are willing to take chances."

"I see." The Chief of the F.B.I. acquired a sudden, faraway look in his eyes. "Maybe I can help you after all. I have one man free in San Diego at the moment, and two in Oakland—"

"Please!" the general cut in quickly. "You don't understand the gravity of the situation. When I said two dozen, I meant just that."

"These three men," the Chief of the F.B.I. went on imperturbably, "are—Kerrigan, Murdoch and Klaw."

The general's eyes flickered for a moment. "I see.... The Suicide Squad." His fingers drummed on the glass desk-top momentarily. "But they may be throwing away their lives."

"That," said the Chief, "is what they've been trying to do right along. So far, they're still hale and healthy."

"You think then that they'd be willing to do it? To go against the whole damned Gestapo. One false step might cause them to be wiped out in an instant."

The Chief smiled. "I rather think they will accept the assignment—when I've made plain the danger involved."

"All right then," said the general. "I'll insert a coded advertisement in the personal column of the Coast City *Courier*, advising Petrie that Kerrigan will contact him at the specified time."

IN A hotel room in San Diego, Johnny Kerrigan heard his

phone ring. He came out of the bathroom where he had been shaving, picked up the phone.

"Johnny," said a voice, "do you know who this is?"

Kerrigan's eyes suddenly gleamed and his teeth flashed in a quick grin.

"Ah!" he said. "I've been hanging around here all day, waiting for a call from you."

"Go downstairs, Johnny, and phone me on my private line, from a foolproof booth. I have something for you and your pals."

Kerrigan hung up, finished his shaving in record time and went downstairs. He found a booth in a small cigar store, and called a certain number in Washington, from memory. Immediately, the same voice answered.

"All right, sir," said Kerrigan. "I'm ready."

"This is an SOS from Military Intelligence, Johnny. There's a man named Petrie in Coast City. You're to contact him at three-thirty tomorrow. You can make it with time to spare. Dan and Steve are flying in from Oakland, but they won't reach Coast City till five o'clock. I've reserved a room for them at the Coast Hotel. Get in touch with them there. The three of you are to give Petrie any assistance he requires. It seems he's on to something pretty big. It's outside the jurisdiction of the Military, yet it isn't a civil crime, either."

"Sounds like a riddle."

"It's a folderol called diplomatic immunity. It may require drastic action not sanctioned by law—"

Johnny Kerrigan grinned into the phone. "I never heard of the law," he said, "What's it?"

"Something that won't help you if you get in trouble. You'll be disowned, repudiated and prosecuted, if you're caught doing anything illegal—provided you're alive. It's your own private war. So the idea is—don't get caught."

"Check," said Johnny, "Where do I contact this Petrie?"

"At Seventh and Myrtle, in Coast City…. Have you got the list of Military Intelligence identification codes?"

"Yes, sir."

"Use Number Fourteen then. Good luck, and God help you."

Johnny grinned once more. "Thank you, sir. God helps those who help themselves!"

AT TEN o'clock the next morning, a man named Horst Keppler was sitting in a room in an office building on the main street of Coast City, half a block away from the German Consulate building.

This man Keppler was tall and distinguished, the very picture of a diplomat. His waxed moustache added the dignity his position as the newly appointed Vice Consul of the German Consulate required—and it served to hide the thin and merciless line of his lips. This office in which he now sat was not connected with the Consulate; it was not even known to the regular consulate staff.

Horst Keppler was talking to another man, who was bending over his desk. This other man was fattish, with a pudgy face and a pair of sly eyes that hid themselves behind thick spectacles. On the roster of the Gestapo, he was listed as *Herr Doktor* Fritz Albrecht, but in other countries he was known by other names. Coast City knew him as Professor Harold Cornish, and he was supposed to be a Swiss mechanical engineer in the employ of the Lane Locomotive Works. But the accomplishments of Professor Harold Cornish, alias *Doktor* Fritz Albrecht, went far beyond those of engineering.

At this moment, he was demonstrating one of those accomplishments to Keppler.

They had a newspaper spread before them. A copy of the morning edition of the Coast City *Courier*. It was opened to the personal column. Albrecht—or Cornish, as he preferred to be called, for the time being—held a thick finger on the personal item which read:

> Roger: Mother madder bit gracious. Kerrigan belongs gamma cold tonight. Good luck.

Albrecht's small eyes were glittering. "It was difficult to break down the code which Petrie sent yesterday, but this one is easier, *Herr* Keppler."

Keppler grunted. "The Americans are fools. They still do not understand the meaning of total war. In our country, a telegraph office would not be left unguarded. It was easy for my men to break in there last night after they closed, and to copy the only coded message in their files for the day."

"I hope your men left no trace of their visit?"

Keppler smiled. "My men are experts, do not fear."

"That is good. So, we know that Petrie sent a call for help to Jason Wellington, the Military Intelligence undercover man in Washington. We know they are aware that Wellington's wire is tapped."

Keppler glanced down at the personal item in the *Courier*. "This, then, is their answer to Petrie? It is in the same code?"

"The same general code, with minor changes. It was not difficult, as I said. Here is the translation."

He produced a slip of paper from his pocket, on which was written:

> Petrie: The Chief has arranged for the Suicide Squad to help
> you. Kerrigan will contact you at the time and place specified.

"I see," said Keppler. "The Suicide Squad. They have always been a thorn in our side, *nicht wahr?*"

"Yes, yes. But today is their last day. They come to their death. You must allow nothing to interfere with our objective in Coast City. We must cripple or destroy the Lane Locomotive Works, which is making heavy tanks for the British."

"Our plans cannot fail. They have been well conceived—" Keppler inclined his head toward the other—"thanks to your genius, *Herr Doktor.*"

Albrecht waved the praise aside. His little eyes had become almost fanatical. "There is another who must also die."

Keppler nodded. "My esteemed chief, the Consul?"

"Exactly. Johann Strang is out of sympathy with our cause. His son, Paul, has gone to an American university, and is more American than German. Strang—or his son—is quite capable of betraying us."

"I shall see that it is taken care of, *Herr Doktor,*" Keppler said softly.

"And you, *Herr* Keppler, shall be promoted from vice-consul to consul. Let us hope that this will be only one small step in your career. Some day, who can tell—" the small eyes became dreamy—"you may even be my assistant—when I am the Deputy-*Fuehrer* of America!"

Albrecht straightened suddenly. "And now, *Herr* Keppler, I leave you. I have important business. I must make all arrangements at the Lane Locomotive Works."

He strode to the door, stopped for a parting admonition. "Do not underestimate this Suicide Squad. You must make very sure that they die today."

"Have no fears, *Herr Doktor*," Keppler told him. "Erase the Suicide Squad from your mind—consider them dead. I stake my life upon it!"

CHAPTER 2
MURDER IN THE DARK

JOHNNY KERRIGAN stopped at the corner and looked around.

The girl in the tan pullover sweater and the short sport skirt was still following him, with a covered tennis racket under her arm. He had noticed her when he got off the train, only a half hour ago. She was not furtive, nor did she seem to be making any effort to conceal the fact that she was tailing him. Indeed, had she wanted to attract attention to herself, she could not have succeeded better than by wearing sport clothes and carrying a tennis racket down here in this queasy slum section of Coast City.

Johnny saw her stop, perhaps fifty feet behind him. The later afternoon sun glinted on her auburn hair. Passing men turned to give her a second glance. But she paid no attention. Her eyes did not leave Johnny Kerrigan.

Johnny frowned, and glanced at his wrist watch. It was exactly three-thirty. He lit a cigarette, then stood there, absently fingering the matchbook, the cigarette hanging from his lips. Idly, his fingers tore the matchbook cover; he began to pluck out the remaining matches one by one, and drop them at his feet.

A seedy-looking bum with a three-day growth of dark beard had been wandering aimlessly near the curb, looking for discarded butts in the gutter. The bum approached Johnny.

"How about a lift for the needy?" he asked.

Johnny looked at him impersonally. "It's raining in England today," he said.

The bum's eyes flickered. "Yes," he replied. "It's raining bombs in England. Stukas. You're Johnny Kerrigan."

"And you're Petrie, of Military Intelligence…. Be careful. I've been followed from the station. Don't look now. It's that girl in the tan sweater."

"I spotted her," Petrie told him. "Her name is Ellen Lane. Her farther owns the Lane Locomotive Works."

Kerrigan whistled, "What's brewing?"

"We can't talk here any longer," Petrie broke in. "They've spotted me. They know who I am, but I think I've given them the slip temporarily. If I haven't, I'm a goner—and you, too. But we'll soon find out. Meet me in twenty minutes in the East End Theatre. It's a cheap movie house two blocks west. Ten cents admission. It won't look too strange for a bum who's just made a touch to blow a dime on a movie. I'll be in the last row on the right-hand side. Sit down next to me. But don't talk to me till I speak first."

Petrie had spoken swiftly. Now he raised his hand. "Slip me a coin to make this look real. We've talked here too long as it is!"

The Military Intelligence man whined his thanks as Kerrigan gave him a quarter. Petrie walked away.

Johnny lit another cigarette with his last remaining match, and looked around, as if he were expecting to meet someone who was late. Out of the corner of his eye he saw the girl in the tan sweater approaching him—Ellen Lane—the daughter of the millionaire locomotive manufacturer, Parker Lane.

She came alongside of him, and her level blue eyes looked up into his gray ones. She was not smiling.

"You're Kerrigan, aren't you?" she asked tautly.

Johnny feigned surprise. "I beg your pardon, Miss?"

She made a gesture of impatience with her free hand. "Please—please don't deny it. You were pointed out to me at the station. I can't be mistaken."

"I'm sorry, Miss," Johnny said, smiling. "You must have mixed up with someone else."

"Stop it!" she said, her voice rising a bit. "You must listen to me. You came here to meet a lieutenant of Military Intelligence. I want to warn you that the appointment will not be kept. That lieutenant of Military Intelligence is dead. Get out of town before they kill you, too!"

Johnny said, "If this is a practical joke, all right. But if you're serious, you better find this Kerrigan that you think I am. *My name happens to be Smith.*"

"Oh, you fool!" She turned away from him swiftly. Then she turned back, and stretched out an impulsive hand. "Please—believe me, I'm telling you the truth. Your life is in danger. *They* know whom you've come to meet. *They* won't let you get farther than any of the others. At least, if you won't go away, be careful!"

Then she swung on her heel and hurried off.

Johnny let her go. He made no attempt to stop her, to question her further. But his eyes were thoughtful as he inhaled the cigarette smoke. And he was watchful. He turned and walked slowly away toward the river front, in the opposite direction from that taken by the girl in the tan sweater.

At the next corner he turned left, entered a subway station. A train was just pulling in. He boarded it, watching behind him to make certain that no one had followed him. He rode two stations, got out and took a taxicab back down to the east side. He got off a block from the East End Theatre, and walked the rest of the way. He was right on time. It was just twenty minutes since Petrie had left him.

He bought a ticket and went inside, into the darkness of the movie house. They were showing a newsreel.

Johnny waited until his eyes were more accustomed to the lack of light, then found his way to the right-hand side. He spotted the figure of Petrie, sitting in the last row, and slid into the folding wooden seat immediately beside him.

He waited a couple of minutes, but Petrie didn't speak.

Johnny looked around, noting that there was no one near

them. He stole a look at the Military Intelligence man, then stiffened, his eyes suddenly hard.

Petrie's head was slumped on his chest. His arms hung limply at his sides. A knife protruded from the back of his neck, the handle supporting Petrie's body, keeping him almost erect.

Petrie's account was closed on the Books. The luminous dial of Johnny Kerrigan's watch showed: Three-fifty-one....

KERRIGAN SAT very still in the dark wondering if the killer was still in the theatre. Watching the audience, he could discern no heads turned to look at him. But he had that universal instinct of the fighting man for scenting danger, the definite sensation of being watched.

Slowly, he reached out and touched Petrie's hand. His fingers found something clutched in Petrie's fist. It was a pencil.

Kerrigan's eyes narrowed. He produced a small, bull's-eye flashlight from his vest pocket and flicked the light on directing the beam first at the back of the seat in front. His guess was correct. Petrie had scribbled a message of warning for him. It was fairly legible:

> *"They have me trapped in here—killers inside and a machine-gun outside. They won't let me leave here alive. If I'm dead when you arrive, go to 23 Slocum Street. Knock twice, then three times. Give the password, AMERICA FOREVER. You can trust the person you will meet there. Don't let them get you!"*

Johnny doused the flashlight, and set about erasing the lower part of the message. Petrie must have been at the end of his rope, to have risked leaving that address and password written there, hoping that Kerrigan would be the first to find it. But Johnny couldn't know, now, whether the killers had seen it too. If so, they would be at 23 Slocum Street before him—

He heard a swift, scraping movement behind him.

Johnny Kerrigan was big, the biggest of the trio of fighting men who were known as the Suicide Squad. He towered head and shoulders above Stephen Klaw, and he topped Dan Murdoch comfortably. His wide, stevedore's shoulders, the solid massiveness of his frame might have given the impression that he was a slow man on his feet, and perhaps a slow thinker.

Nothing could have been farther from the truth. Where a question of physical combat arose, Kerrigan reacted with the split-second timing which is second nature to men who live with danger.

That scraping sound of leather sole upon hardwood floor at his back had hardly reached his ears before he threw himself forward and to the right, in a twisting, snake-like motion.

Something swished viciously down past his shoulder blades, and then there was a dull thwack as a knife-point embedded itself in the veneer of the wooden bench upon which he had been sitting.

Johnny swung around to face the killer who had driven the knife. The man was a powerful fellow, almost as big as Johnny himself. He was wearing a soft hat like Kerrigan's, and thin kid gloves. It was his gloved right hand which held the knife.

The attacker's eyes glittered in the dark as he yanked at the handle, desperately yanking it out of the wood for another attempt.

Kerrigan's laugh was soft, lost in the overtones of the newsreel sounds. On the screen they were showing the goose-stepping march of Nazi troops through the Balkans, with the hob-nailed shoes resounding in regimented unison upon the cobbled streets of a once-peaceful village.

And strangely enough, that clatter of Nasi boots in the village five thousand miles away was to have a deciding effect upon the fortunes of the Nazi plans here in America. In covering the sounds of the struggle there in the back of the East End Theatre, it contributed no little to the events that followed.

The struggle was one of life and death, with no quarter asked or given. And it was silent, because Kerrigan's big right hand drove out to grasp the knife-man's throat with fingers of steel, while his left seized the assailant's right wrist.

The two men stood chest to chest across the narrow back of the bench, straining in mortal combat. The knife-man's muscles bulged with the effort to push his blade home against Johnny's grip on his wrist, while Johnny grimly kept his hold on the killer's throat, his thumb pressing against the windpipe.

It was a struggle of muscle against muscle, of body against body, with every ounce of strength and will thrown into the scales, and death for the loser.

KERRIGAN GRUNTED, let go his hold on the thick throat, and seized the knife-wrist in both hands. He jerked downward, and a gasp of pain escaped from the man's lips as the bone cracked. He dropped the dagger.

Johnny let go of him, vaulted over the back of the seat, and caught him by the coat just as he was turning to run.

The fellow snarled, stooped and snatched up the knife in his left hand, tried to slash with it. Johnny stepped in again, and smashed home a left and a right to his face, rocking him back off balance so that the knife could not be swung. The fellow turned to run, heading for the exit at the side.

Johnny started after him, but the man was already at the exit door. He ripped it open, and leaped out into the alley.

Kerrigan was only a couple of feet behind him, coming fast. Abruptly, he heard a sound which slapped against his eardrums with the dread familiarity of doom. It was the sound of a machine-gun, beginning its deadly stutter of death.

Johnny stopped short, remaining just inside the theatre, out of the line of fire of that deadly spray of bullets in the alley.

But the other man was already out in the open, facing the gun. Johnny saw the flashing, spitting muzzle of the machine-gun, farther up the alley, toward the street. Petrie had warned him of this. The knife-man must have known about it too, but he was probably dazed by his broken wrist, confused and panic-stricken at his failure.

Whatever the cause of his error, the knife-man was paying for it with his life. He was the same build as Kerrigan, and he wore the same kind of hat. That gunner out there must have been sure that it was Kerrigan. The spray of machine-gun bullets was a little high, but not too high to miss the knife-man....

Almost before the machine-gun ceased its chattering clatter of destruction, Johnny Kerrigan was out in the alley, with a big service revolver in his hand. He glimpsed the figure of the machine-gunner slinging the weapon to his shoulder and turning to run toward a car parked out at the curb, in front of the alley's mouth.

Instinctively Johnny raised his gun. The machine-gunner was an easy mark—Johnny had only to pull the trigger. But his eyes narrowed; and he lowered the gun without firing, an idea growing into a plan within his brain.

He made no attempt to stop the fleeing car into which the machine-gunner had leaped. Instead, he knelt swiftly beside the dead killer, and went through his pockets. The man had removed all identifying marks from his clothing, as well as all objects from his pockets.

Kerrigan took off his own hat and dropped it beside the dead body, picking up the knife-man's hat in exchange. It had fallen from the fellow's head as he had stumbled out into the alley, and had consequently escaped a riddling. It was in serviceable shape.

Johnny thrust the hat on his head, and dashed out of the alley. He heard shouts from the theatre, where the audience had finally awakened to the fact that a real struggle had been taking place right behind their backs. But there was no rush of people out into the alley. They had heard the chopping machine-gun, and they had no desire to court its chattering attention.

Kerrigan ducked down the street, crossed to the other side and disappeared into another alley, just as a uniformed police-man came pounding down from the corner.

Kerrigan stood in the shadows for a moment. The officer, fortunately, had not noticed him.

Johnny found a cab and climbed into it, ordering the driver uptown to Slocum Street. As they pulled away to the accompaniment of the sirens, Kerrigan nodded in bleak satisfaction. That knife-man was no longer recognizable, and he was lying there with Kerrigan's hat beside him—a hat with the initials, JK, in the band, and the maker's name plainly stamped on the label. That dead man would be assumed to be one, Kerrigan, of the Federal Bureau of Investigation. Johnny intended to make the most of that piece of good luck.

CHAPTER 3
THE LADY AND THE GUN

S LOCUM STREET was residential. It was an old, conservative street, with no great apartment houses. At one time, the aristocracy of the city had lived here. Now these rambling old houses set back from the street, shaded by venerable elms, were a bit seedy and run down, with peeling paint and patched roofs. Several of them had "Furnished Rooms" signs, and on the ground floor of Number 23 there was a modest card:

STELLA LAWRENCE
Dressmaker

Kerrigan had his cabby drive past the house without stopping. He got out at the next corner, his keen eyes scanning both sides of the street. He was not yet sure whether that message left by Petrie on the back of the motion picture theatre seat had been seen by anyone else. If it had, then 23 Slocum Street would be covered.

But he could spot nobody in the street, nor could he see anyone lurking at the windows of the neighboring houses.

He walked back from the corner, turned into the flagstone path, and went up the three steps of the porch to the door. Another card over the bell just gave the name of Stella Lawrence.

Kerrigan didn't ring the bell. He remembered, as if it was etched indelibly in his brain, Petrie's death-message: *Knock twice, then three times.*

If Petrie had said knock, that was what he had meant. But if Petrie's killers had written that message after killing the Military Intelligence man, that signal might be a trap. It was conceivable that the killers had written the message. Kerrigan knew how thorough were the men with whom he had to deal. They made their plans carefully, and then, just to make doubly sure, they made another, supplementary set of plans, in case the first one failed.

He shrugged, raised his hand, and rapped the signal.

He waited, outwardly at ease, inwardly keyed to the steel-spring tension that could erupt into lightning-like action.

From within came the sound of movement, close to the door. A bolt scraped back. The knob turned, and the door opened wide.

Kerrigan looked into a dim hall, from which all light had been excluded.

Facing him, about five feet from the door, was the girl in the tan sweater.

She looked just as she had looked earlier. She was still holding that covered tennis racket under her arm.

22

"Come in," she said.

Johnny Kerrigan didn't move. His eyes swept down the hall behind her, to the open doorway that led into a living-room. He could discern no sign of life in there, but he noted that she was five feet from the door. She could not have opened it and stepped back that far. Someone else had opened the door—someone who waited behind the door.

"Good afternoon, Miss Lane," Johnny said, still not moving.

Her eyes flickered. She moved the tennis racket a little. It was resting under her arm, with the wide part close to her body and the handle poking out to the front.

Kerrigan's blood raced as he noted that the end of that handle was not covered. And it was not wood. It was a round, open muzzle! Inside that cover was no tennis racket, but a small sub-machine gun!

The girl was breathing fast as she pointed the disguised gun.

"Come in," she repeated.

"Sure," said Kerrigan. "Always glad to oblige a lady."

He started forward, threw himself into a low tackle, and hurtled the short distance between them like a driving catapult.

The girl uttered a startled cry. "Paul! Help!"

SHE COULD have pulled the trigger and sent a blasting hail of slugs into Kerrigan's body; but his motions had been utterly deceptive. His slow drawl and his even slower start had caught her off guard. And his quick switch to blinding action had taken her completely by surprise. In the second which she needed to ready herself, he struck her, winding his arms around her waist and carrying her backward with him.

Kerrigan swung her off her feet, snatched the machine-gun from her and threw it into a corner. Then he drew his revolver, and swung to face the door, holding her struggling body close to him.

He leveled his gun at the young man who had been hiding behind the door, with an automatic pistol in his hand.

"All right, sport," said Johnny. "Start shooting any time you like."

The young fellow was tall, hardly more than twenty-five or twenty-six, with blond hair and light blue eyes.

He said, "Let go of Ellen!"

"Put down the gun, sport, and I'll let her go."

"Put it down, Paul," the girl said tiredly. "He'll kill you."

"Let him kill me. I don't care any more. He'll kill us both anyway."

"You're crazy," Johnny said. "I won't kill either of you. I don't kill kids. I leave that to the Nazis."

The boy's eyes opened wide. "You—you're not—one of Keppler's men?"

Kerrigan laughed harshly. "Ask your girl friend. She knows me. She called me by name this afternoon."

"Put the gun away, Paul," the girl repeated. "And close the door. Let's talk to him. I think we've made a mistake."

The blond young man hesitated, watching Kerrigan covertly.

Johnny grinned. He kept his hold on the girl, but he replaced his revolver in its holster.

"There!" he said. "How's that for disarmament?"

24

Paul slowly lowered his own automatic, and put it in his pocket.

"Let's go inside," Ellen said, and led the way.

In the living-room, the radio was turned on low, to the news reports. Paul put his arm around the girl's shoulders, and they both faced Johnny Kerrigan, studying him, not quite sure of themselves.

"Well?" asked the girl.

"You came over to me today, at the corner of Seventh and Myrtle," Kerrigan said. "You called me by name, warned me to go away. You told me that Petrie, the Military Intelligence man, had been killed."

"Yes," she said. "I told you that."

"How did you know?"

"Before I answer that," she said, "I want to know if you're really Kerrigan. Prove to me that you're Kerrigan."

Johnny took an identification card case from his pocket, flipped it open, and showed it to her. Paul peered down at it carefully, studying the picture and comparing it with Johnny's features.

"He's Kerrigan, all right," he said.

Suddenly the girl smiled. "I was sure you were Kerrigan, but after I talked to you at the corner of Seventh and Myrtle, I thought perhaps I'd been mistaken. You see, I stood right behind two men at the railroad station who were watching for you. I heard one of them tell the other who you were, and that they were not to follow you, because they knew just where you were going. He said you were to meet a man named Petrie at the corner of Seventh and Myrtle, and that you would be followed from there."

"Tell me more about this," Johnny said grimly. "Who were those men?"

"Two agents of the Gestapo here in Coast City."

THE GIRL glanced inquiringly at Paul.

He nodded. "I think it's safe to tell him. Go ahead."

She looked back at Johnny. "I'm Ellen Lane. This is Paul Strang. We're engaged. He's the son of Johann Strang, the German Consul here. His father hates the Nazis. He has refused to cooperate with them. He told Paul a little of what was going on, and Paul told me. There's a man named Fritz Albrecht here in Coast City—a terrible man. He's in charge of all sabotage work in America. They must be plotting something tremendous to bring him here in person. What it is, we don't know. But we *do* know that Paul's father's life is in danger. We also know that they got hold of the message that Petrie sent to his headquarters, and that they decoded an ad in the personal column of the *Courier*. They killed Petrie, and they were going to wait till you met your two friends, Murdoch and Klaw, and kill the three of you at once—"

"Just a minute," Johnny interrupted. "You told me before that they had killed Petrie. When did this happen?"

"This morning at eleven o'clock."

"You're sure?"

"Of course we're sure. They killed him out in back of Paul's father's house. They shot him with a machine-gun."

Johnny nodded. "Then Petrie couldn't have met me this afternoon at three-thirty—"

"That's what Ellen's been trying to tell you!" Paul Strang exclaimed.

"What would you say," Kerrigan asked them, "if I told you that I did meet Petrie at three-thirty?"

"Impossible!" said Paul. "My dad went out of town on a secret mission, and while he was out, Petrie called up and said he was coming over—about something important. Dad was working secretly with Petrie, giving him information about Nazi activities. It was because of the information my dad gave him, that Petrie wired Washington for help."

He paused, his arm tightening around Ellen. "Well, Ellen and I waited up for Petrie. We watched for him through the back window of the upstairs bedroom. He was supposed to come in through the rear. We saw him coming across the open lot, from the back street, and then we saw the car coming along the street behind him. He was too far away for us to warn him. Someone stuck a machine-gun out of the car and blasted away. Then the car streaked away."

"Did you see Petrie's face?" Kerrigan asked.

"No. He was too far away. But it was his build, and we were expecting him."

"I'm sorry," said Johnny. "It wasn't Petrie who was killed this morning. I met him. He was killed all right—but not till four o'clock this afternoon!"

The faces of the boy and girl were suddenly white. "Then— then who—"

"I hate to ask this," Kerrigan said slowly, looking Paul Strang squarely in the eyes. "But—what did your father look like? Was his general build the same as Petrie's? Could you have mistaken your father for Petrie?"

He had his answer in the sudden ghastly look of pain in the boy's eyes.

"Yes!" Paul whispered. "God help me, I could have been mistaken!"

"I'm sorry," Johnny said.

The boy's face suddenly hardened, his blue eyes flashed. "They knew they were killing dad! The beasts! They had to get rid of him, so he wouldn't spoil their plans. Well, they haven't heard the last from the Strangs! I'm an American! I have my citizenship papers. With dad dead, I'm not afraid of them any more. By God, I'm going to avenge my father if it means killing the whole damned Nazi crew!"

"I'm with you, Paul!" the girl whispered.

Just then, the voice on the radio changed. A local newscaster came on. Ellen hurried over, and turned the volume up. The announcer was saying:

Two more killings have quickly followed the murder of the unidentified man who was machine-gunned this morning, behind the home of the German Consul. This time, one man was stabbed to death in a motion picture theatre, and the other was blasted by a machine-gun, in the same manner as the morning's victim. Police are at a loss to assign a motive for these killings. No identification was found on this morning's victim, or on the body of the man who was stabbed. But the man who met his death by machine-gun fire in an alley beside the East End Theatre has been identified by his hat. It contained initials and a Washington men's clothing store address. Through this address, it has been established that the victim is John Kerrigan, an F.B.I. agent...."

Ellen Lane and Paul Strang turned to look at Johnny.

Kerrigan chuckled. "Don't believe everything you hear. Those boys wanted me dead, so I obliged by leaving my hat. Now let's get out of here."

"Where?" demanded Ellen.

"To the Coast Hotel. My two friends ought to be in by this time. They'll be interested to meet my corpse!"

CHAPTER 4
"YOU CAN'T KILL A G-MAN"

I N ROOM 504 of the Coast Hotel, Dan Murdoch snapped off the radio, and stood for a moment with his hand on the knob. His eyes were fixed blankly on the wall. Then he turned around slowly and faced his partner, Stephen Klaw.

"I don't believe it!" he said hoarsely. "Johnny wouldn't let them shoot his head off with a machine-gun—like any dumb lug!"

Stephen Klaw sat very stiff and straight in his chair.

"We have to find out, Dan," he said. "We have to find out if that was really Johnny." He got up, went to the window, and pulled the blind back a little. He peered out through the crack.

"One of the two guys who followed us from the airport is

out there across the street, watching this window. The other one must be downstairs in the lobby."

"Let's find out from them," Murdoch said. "Let's bring one of them up here, and—"

"No. If Johnny's dead, he'd want us to carry on. We've got to find out what Petrie had to tell him. If Petrie's dead too, then we must find out some other way. Johnny'd want us to clean up for him."

These two—the other two-thirds of the Suicide Squad—were not ones to show emotion. But each knew how the other felt. They had come a long way together, the three of them. Their lives, individually and severally, were long ago forfeit to the laws of chance and the odds on death. It was their job to pull the beard of the Grim Reaper. Not for nothing were they known as the Suicide Squad. They never got a routine job, but were kept in reserve for the cases which called for their particular qualities—reckless daring and a total disregard for personal safety. It was the way they wanted it.

Once there had been five men in the Suicide Squad. Then only four. Then three.

Now, Murdoch and Klaw sat in this hotel room and wondered whether they were only two. Tomorrow, there might be only one—or none.

Johnny Kerrigan had once punched a senator's son in the nose; Dan Murdoch had once shot a croupier to death in a crooked gambling house; Stephen Klaw had once told a Senate Investigating Committee chairman to go to hell when he had been asked why he had shot to kill, in a gun battle with bandits.

Such offenses would have brought about the immediate discharge of any other F.B.I. men. But such was the record of these three, public resentment would have been raised at their dismissal. The Chief of the F.B.I. had used this argument to good advantage on several occasions in refusing to fire them.

He had been allowed to keep them in service on the condition that they were never given ordinary assignments, where they might come in contact with the powers-that-be. So they got only those jobs which the Chief hesitated to assign, or even to ask for volunteers. They took the jobs gratefully, because it was in their nature to seek that kind of danger. They would have been unhappy—without Death at their elbows.

They had always hoped the end would come for all three of them together; shoulder to shoulder, they'd go down with blazing guns.

"If they really got him," Stephen Klaw said tightly, "we'll give them a show they'll never forget!"

They had just gotten into the hotel a few minutes ago, without baggage. When the Suicide Squad was working on an assignment, they never carried baggage. They worked without benefit of laundry. Theirs was a simple system: they bought fresh clothes, and gave away the dirty. In this way they were never hampered by possessions. Their salary, plus their expense account, adequately covered this unique method of working. Though they never bothered to submit an expense account, the Chief of the F.B.I. thoughtfully issued generous vouchers for them whenever he figured they needed money. For money was the last thing in the world to which Kerrigan, Murdoch and Klaw ever gave any consideration.

Dan Murdoch had come up alongside Steve, and was peering cautiously out the window.

"Well," he said. "It looks like somebody in the hotel is getting company!" A police car had pulled in to the opposite curb. Two plain-clothes men and two uniformed policemen had descended from it. They were crossing toward the hotel.

"I don't like the looks of it," Steve muttered. "They could be coming for us."

"The police in this town are supposed to be okay," said Murdoch.

"Yes. But we ought to play it safe."

"The next room is vacant," said Murdoch. "I saw the key in the reservation box. One of us could cover from there—"

"You do it, Dan."

Murdoch shrugged. He took a set of passkeys from his pocket, and went to the connecting door. In a moment he was through, into the next room.

He wasn't any too soon, for almost at once a knock sounded on the corridor door.

"Open, in the name of the law!"

STEPHEN KLAW'S eyes became dark and hot. "Close the door, Dan."

As soon as Murdoch had closed the connecting door between them, Klaw went to the corridor door.

"Who is it?" he asked.

"Open up," said a voice. "This is Captain Warren of Homicide!"

Steve opened the door.

The headquarters men who had descended from the police car were grouped close to the door. Captain Warren was a large, florid man, with a pair of keen gray eyes. He showed his badge and stepped in, followed by the plain-clothes man and the two uniformed policemen. He eyed Steve carefully.

Klaw was slim and wiry, so youthful in appearance that he could have been mistaken for a college kid on vacation. Few people, looking at him, realized that his compact frame carried one hundred and sixty pounds of bone and muscle.

Captain Warren said, "You don't look like a murderer."

Steve raised his eyebrows. "Murderer?"

Warren motioned to the plain-clothes man beside him. "This is Sergeant Rand, also of Homicide." His eyes strayed around the room. "I thought there were two of you."

"There were," said Steve.

"What happened to the other fellow?"

"I murdered him."

"Now don't get funny!" Captain Warren barked. "How long you been in town?"

"You're asking too many questions," Steve replied. "Suppose I ask one. What are you doing here?"

"We're after a couple of murderers," Warren told him, suddenly smooth again. "We were tipped off that the two killers who machine-gunned that man at the theatre were hiding out in this room. Whoever did that job also pulled the one this morning, near the German consul's house. Anything you say may be used against you—"

"Thank you," said Steve. His eyes were bright and hot. He was being accused of having murdered Johnny Kerrigan! "Of course, if that's the case, I'll answer any questions you have to ask."

"You had a friend with you. Where is he?"

"He left for Alaska five minutes ago—"

Sergeant Rand broke in angrily. "He's one of these wise-guys, Captain. Let's take him in—"

Warren raised a hand. "Wait!" He was watching Steve. "All right, never mind your friend for the moment. What time did you get in town?"

"We checked into the hotel at exactly three-fifty-nine. You can check at the desk."

Warren nodded. "Time enough to knock off that guy at the theatre and to get here."

"That's right," said Steve.

"Where do you come from?"

"Oakland, last."

"What's your business?"

"I'm in the exterminating business," Steve told him. "I exterminate rats."

Sergeant Rand uttered a short, barking laugh. "How do you get rid of them? With machine-guns?"

Warren nodded to the two uniformed men. "Go through the room. See what you can find."

"I have no baggage," Steve said.

"I can see that," Warren observed. "It's not baggage we're looking for."

From the bathroom, came the voice of one of the cops. "Here it is, Captain!"

He came out with an extremely long and narrow suitcase. "It was in the bathtub, hidden by the shower sheet."

The cop put the suitcase on the floor and snapped the catch. The lid came open, revealing a shiny, well-oiled machine-gun!

"Well," said Captain Warren. "What's your story?"

"Offhand," Steve replied, "I'd say that you planted it here."

Warren's face flushed. "You little squirt—" He took a step forward, raising a fist.

Steve didn't give an inch. He looked up into Warren's face, smiling thinly, tightly. "Yes, Captain?"

Warren stopped short, his fist still raised. "You're lucky I don't believe in roughhouse!" he growled.

"Lucky?" Steve retorted. "With a machine-gun planted in my room? And a murder rap tied to it?"

WARREN FROWNED, studying him closely. "There is something smelly about this. You're just a kid. You don't look like a hopped-up gunman who'd work a chopper as cold-bloodedly as this one was worked."

"Thank you, Captain. Do you mind telling me how you knew about that gun?"

"We were tipped off. Anonymously."

"Then this could be a frame?"

"Sure it could. But you're not helping yourself much. What time did you get into town?"

"At three-thirty-seven, from an airliner at the airport."

"Did you come straight here?"

"No, we walked around the town a little, to get acquainted with it."

"So you can't show an alibi for three-fifty-one?"

"I'm sorry, no."

"Well, who are you?"

That was a question Steve couldn't answer. He couldn't say that he was an agent of the Federal Bureau of Investigation, here on official business. Because the Chief had told him, as he had told Kerrigan, that this was to be the Suicide Squad's private war. They were here on official business, all right—but unofficially.

"The name is Klaw," he said. "S. Klaw."

"I know that!" Warren growled impatiently. "It's on the register downstairs. It doesn't mean a thing to me. Tell me more, if you're interested in beating this rap. I'd like to help you, but you're not making it easy."

"I'm sorry, Captain," Steve said sincerely. "I really appreciate the way you're handling this. But there's no more I can tell you."

Warren shrugged. "In that case, I'll have to take you in. I haven't any choice but—"

Suddenly, from out in the hall, there came a wild, frantic scream, followed by a high-pitched shout.

"Help! They're killing me! Help!"

The cry was drowned out by two thunderous revolver shots. The echo of the shots rolled away, and was followed by the slamming of a door somewhere out in the corridor.

Everybody in the room sprang to attention. Warren swung

toward the door, followed by Rand and the two cops. For the moment, Stephen Klaw was forgotten.

"It's a killing!" Warren shouted. "Let's go!"

He tore open the corridor door and dashed out, drawing his service revolver, with Rand and the others at his heels.

The smell of cordite was pungent in the hall, indicating that the shooting had taken place right out here. But there was no one in sight.

"Spread out!" Warren ordered. "Casey, Wolfe, try every door! Rand, cover the emergency exit! Watch the fire-stairs! I'll cover the hall out here in case he tries to make a break for the elevators."

Inside his room, Stephen Klaw did not seem at all excited to this new activity. He stepped calmly to the corridor door, closed and locked it, then called, "Okay Dan. You can come in."

Dan Murdoch entered grinning, through the connecting door of the next room. A smoking revolver was still in his hand.

"How did I do, Shrimp?"

"Not bad, Mope. That scream was a work of art. And you spaced the shots nicely, too. They'll be looking for a body in every room on the floor."

"Now all we have to do is get out of here," said Murdoch.

He went to the window, opened it.

Steve was already yanking sheets off the bed, and tearing them into strips, then twisting them around and knotting them together. No useless words were spoken, no useless instructions given. They had worked so long together that they could almost read each other's minds; they could tell what the other would do under given conditions. And now, as they made a short rope of the sheets, they thought of Johnny Kerrigan....

There was more to this job than mere personal escape from a trap. Now they had nothing to look forward to but being hunted day and night. It would have been easier to declare their identity to the police, and quit, to wire Washington that events had made it impossible for them to continue; that other men must be sent in their stead.

But that was not the way of the Suicide Squad. They had to find out what had really happened to Kerrigan. They had to square things up for him.

Murdoch fastened one end of the knotted sheet to the radiator, pulling hard at it to make sure it wouldn't give under their weight. Then he threw the other end out of the window. The improvised rope was just long enough to reach the window of the room below.

"You first, Shrimp," he said.

Steve shook his head, and bowed elaborately. "After you...."

They were kibitzing around to cover the much deeper feeling which was gnawing at each of them. Their memories were warm with the incidents of a hundred adventures which three of them had shared together.

"I think I'll take this little toy along with me," Steve said, indicating the suitcase with the machine-gun, which Warren's men had left on the floor. He closed the lid, tied another bit of sheet through the handle and around his waist, so that it hung free. Then he went over the sill.

HAND OVER hand he climbed down to the window below.

Hanging there a moment, four stories above the ground, he peered in through the closed window. There was no one inside. He raised his head and nodded to Murdoch, who was watching from above.

"Snap it up, Shrimp," Murdoch called. "I think your friends are coming back. They must smell a rat."

"Here we go," said Steve.

He lashed out with his right foot, shattering the window pane. Then he swung himself over the ledge, into the room.

A moment later, Dan Murdoch joined him. From above, they could hear someone banging hard at the door of the room they had just left.

"Nice timing," said Murdoch.

Steve untied the valise from around his waist, picked it up. The two of them sauntered out into the corridor.

The hall was full of people, milling around and asking excited questions.

"This is an outrage!" a fat man was saying shrilly. "I thought this was a respectable hotel—"

"So did I!" said Dan Murdoch. "My friend and I refuse to remain here another minute!"

They made their way to the elevator, but there was no escape that way. A small crowd was gathered around the shaft, but the cage was not running.

They hurried past, went around the bend, and made for the fire-exit. They sped down the stairs, Murdoch in the lead. They encountered no one on the third floor or second floor, but on the way down to the main floor they almost ran into Sergeant Rand, who was on his way up, with his service revolver in his hand.

He saw them coining. He raised the gun.

"Stand still!" he shouted. "So it was all a trick—"

Rand was at the foot of the stairs, and Murdoch, a little in advance of Steve, was on the sixth or seventh step. He bent down, doubling up almost into a knot, and literally rolled the rest of the way, straight at Rand.

The sergeant cursed, and lowered his revolver for a shot at Murdoch. But something came sailing through the air and struck him on the shoulder with irresistible velocity. It was Steve Klaw's valise that had appeared as though shot from a catapult.

With uncanny timing—almost as if he had known exactly what Dan was going to do—Steve had slung that valise.

The sergeant staggered backward, without firing his gun. Dan Murdoch got in front of him, smiling apologetically.

"I regret this exceedingly, Sergeant," Dan said in that suave way of his, and drove a hard fist to Rand's jaw. The blow scarcely traveled five inches.

Rand went down, cold. Murdoch rubbed his knuckles. "The sergeant has a pretty tough jaw. Remind me to apologize to him sometime."

Steve picked up the valise again. "So far, you're batting a thousand, Mope. Let's go!

They left Rand lying on the floor, and went out through the emergency fire door, into the alley alongside the hotel.

There was a lot of excitement out in the street. A siren was playing a wild dirge, and people were crowding toward the hotel entrance, around the two police cars which were pulling up.

Murdoch and Klaw stepped out into the crowd unobserved.

"Which way do we go, Dan?" Steve asked. "East or west?"

"I think," Dan Murdock said in a queer, choked voice, "that we will go across the street and punch somebody square in the nose for giving us gray hairs!"

Steve's eyes glinted joyfully as he followed Dan's glance.

"Thank God!" he whispered, his strong fingers on Dan's shoulder.

There, in a taxicab across the street, right behind a police car, they saw Johnny Kerrigan sitting with Ellen Lane and Paul Strang. Johnny was grinning at them like an Andalusian ape.

CHAPTER 5
SUBSCRIPTION—TO DEATH!

HERR HORST KEPPLER was absently polishing his monocle. He was not any too happy.

"But my dear *Doktor* Albrecht," he said, "you must at least grant that I have accomplished a good deal today. My men have eliminated Johann Strang, who was the most dangerous to our plans, for he knew so much of them. In addition, we have liquidated the Military Intelligence man, Petrie, as well as that Kerrigan."

Professor Harold Cornish, alias *Doktor* Fritz Albrecht, was pacing up and down the secret office. He turned his small eyes, cloaked by the thick-lenses, upon Keppler.

41

"All that is not enough, Keppler. I gave you instructions to eliminate the other two—Murdoch and Klaw."

"That is true, *Doktor* Albrecht. But a peculiar circumstance arose. My chief lieutenant—Max Gussnig—has disappeared. It was he who stabbed Petrie to death in the motion picture theatre, and who also sent Kerrigan, out into the alley where he was cut down by my machine-gunner. But I have not heard from Gussnig since. Perhaps he was spotted by someone at the theatre, and has had to lie low for a while. It was through him that I intended to issue orders to eliminate Murdoch and Klaw. But I've had to handle them in different fashion, by throwing suspicion upon them for the other killings. I had a machine-gun planted in their room, and informed the police."

"But they have escaped, Keppler."

"They are devils, *Herr Doktor*. They are very clever."

"Yes, they are very clever," Albrecht agreed. "We should have men like them working for us. Men who can think quickly in an emergency. Not men who flounder around when the slightest detail goes wrong!"

As he said this he looked directly at Keppler, who grew slightly pale.

"I did my best, *Herr Doktor*—"

"Your best was not enough!"

"And yet, I have succeeded in reducing the danger from those two. They are even now being hunted throughout the city—by their own police. Sooner or later they will be caught. Probably shot on sight."

"Well," growled Albrecht, "I do not feel comfortable while

those daredevils are loose. There is no telling what they will do next. Above all, we must keep them from meeting Paul Strang."

"I am sure they are too busy hiding from the police, to be in a position to contact anyone."

"Well, we shall see. We shall see."

Albrecht picked up a telescope from the desk, and went to the window. From here was afforded a clear view of the eastern end of the town, where the great manufacturing plants of Coast City were located. Dominating all the others was the huge, sprawling layout of the Lane Locomotive Works, spread out over forty acres of land, with huge funnels leaning up into the sky, and red-flecked smoke-plumes seething out in the gathering dusk. There were tremendous blast furnaces, forging and welding shops, and a huge assembly plant which alone covered seven acres.

Swinging his telescope, Albrecht sighted the proving grounds, where tanks were being tested, day and night. After the final okay, these machines of war would be ready for the long voyage to Britain.

Albrecht's pudgy face was working strangely as he studied that great unit of American industrial strength which was forging weapons to oppose the Nazi juggernaut abroad.

"Tonight it shall be destroyed!" he muttered. "Utterly destroyed. Tomorrow there will be no smoke-stacks there, no shops, no men. Nothing!"

He lowered the telescope and swung to face Keppler. His eyes were burning with a frightful, fanatical intensity.

"Our plan must proceed according to schedule. Nothing shall

stop us. For six months I have worked in that plant—studying, planning. I know every nook and corner of the shops, I know its vital parts. Tonight, when I go back to work on the night shift, I shall bring them a present they will never forget!"

KEPPLER WAS awed by the fanaticism of the man. "You cannot fail, *Herr Doktor*. You are too clever for them."

"But you must do your part, Keppler. Do you understand your duties for tonight?"

"Thoroughly, *Herr Doktor*. At six o'clock, when the night shift goes on, the fifty men whom you have supplied with false identification cards and badges, will enter with the other workers. Each will go to the spot which you have designated on the blueprint map of the plant. At each spot there is a flame-thrower, twenty-five of them in all."

"Exactly," said Albrecht. "I made those flame-throwers myself, in that plant, while they thought I was working on their new tank designs. The stupid Americans!"

"They are no match for us," Keppler said smugly.

Albrecht waved impatiently. "Go on. Go on with the plans."

"I will be among those fifty men, of course," Keppler continued. "We will wait until you give the signal. Three sharp blasts of your whistle, followed by two blasts. At the signal, I will lead ten men to the office. There, we will seize the manager and the executive staff. We will also take the tank plans. In the meantime, the *flammenwerfer* will be spreading fire and destruction throughout the plant. We will wait at the gate with our captives until you have set off the secret mine which you placed under the floorboards of your own workshop. Then, we will all leave the plant and escape in the special cars which I have prepared. We will go directly to the beach, where dories will be waiting to take us off to our waiting submarine. We will take the executives with us to Germany, where they will be questioned for the purpose of forcing them to disclose the secret speed-ratios which make their tanks so fast, and which you have been unable to steal."

"Good!" grunted Albrecht. "Also, you must remember that I want the girl, Ellen Lane. She will be there tonight. She comes every night. She must be taken back to Germany with us. Once she is in our hands, we can force her father to become a friend of our cause, instead of a friend of Britain. Parker Lane is an important figure in American life. If he should suddenly change his views, he will command a great following among Americans who admire him. So do not forget the girl!"

"I shall not forget, *Herr Doktor*. She shall be my personal responsibility."

Albrecht was picking up his hat and cane, when a strange look crossed his face. Instead of saying goodbye, he continued to talk in a loud voice. He came over to the desk, snatched up a pencil. Still talking, he wrote: *There is somebody listening at the door!*

Keppler's eyes narrowed. He opened a drawer, and snatched out an automatic. Then, while Albrecht continued his monologue, Keppler stepped over to the door, turned the knob, and pulled it open.

Young Paul Strang stood in the hall.

"What are you doing here?" Keppler demanded.

"I came to see you and *Herr Doktor* Albrecht."

"How did you know I had an office here?"

"I followed you once or twice, when you left the Consulate."

Keppler stepped out in the hall, glancing up and down to make sure Paul was alone. Then he prodded the young man with his gun. "Get in there!"

He pushed Paul roughly into the room.

The *Herr Doktor* threw an acidulous glance at Keppler. "Is this the efficiency with which you operate? You have allowed this young cur to ferret out your secret headquarters!"

Albrecht turned his small eyes upon Paul. "Why have you come here?"

"To talk with you, *Herr Doktor*."

"How do you know who I am?"

"My father told me about you. Last week, we saw you in the street, and he pointed you out to me. He said if ever there was trouble here in Coast City, I could be sure you'd be behind it."

"Ah, so!" said *Doktor* Albrecht. "What is it that you wish to say to me?"

"I want to ask you a question," Paul said. "I want to know why you murdered my father!"

FOR AN instant, the *Herr Doktor* Albrecht was silent. He exchanged a swift glance with Keppler, and then his thick lips wreathed themselves into a smile. "Ah, so! You know that your father is dead. And you believe that it was I who ordered his execution."

"It was murder," Paul said. "This isn't Germany. The laws of Germany don't go here."

"You are mistaken, my young friend," Albrecht replied softly.

"A German is subject to the laws of the Third Reich—wherever he may be. Your father was executed because he was a traitor."

"You mean," Paul said hotly, "that he was murdered because he couldn't stomach your damned Nazi treachery?"

Albrecht shrugged. "Have it your own way. Words will mean nothing when the Third Reich finally triumphs. As for you—the day shall come too late for you to see it."

"You can't kill me, too," Paul exclaimed. "You won't get away with it. My father was a subject of the Third German Reich. But not me. I'm an American citizen. My mother was an American. I'm naturalized. I'm not subject to your laws."

He took a step forward. "I don't know what name you're using here in Coast City, *Herr* Albrecht, but I aim to find out. I intend to find out what it is you're up to, and I'm going to spoil your little game when I do find out!"

"My poor young friend!" Albrecht smiled coldly. "You have talked yourself into an early grave!" He nodded to Keppler, who had reversed his automatic, and was standing just behind Paul. *"Now,* Keppler!"

Herr Keppler started to bring the gun down on Paul's head in a vicious, skull-cracking blow.

But his arm froze in mid-air. A sharp knock sounded at the door.

"Wait!" Albrecht ordered. "I must not be found here. This young fool does not know what name I am using in this city. But someone else may recognize me!"

He stepped close to Keppler and whispered, "I will leave by the side door. Get rid of whoever it is, then dispose of young

Strang. You can leave his body here. After tonight, we will not need this office."

Keppler nodded, his gun digging into Paul's back. Albrecht stepped over to a side door, opened it and slipped out. That door led through another office, into the service corridor; from there he could make his way, unobserved, out of the building.

The knock at the door was repeated.

Frowning, Keppler went and opened it. Dan Murdoch was standing there, holding half a dozen good magazines.

"Good evening," Dan said politely. "Would you be interested in combination subscriptions to America's most popular magazines? We have a special offer—"

"Gott im Himmel!" snarled Keppler.

He started to close the door, but Murdoch had his foot in the opening. "Surely you read magazines, mister? Don't you want to help me work my way through college? Now for two dollars and fifty cents—"

"Get out!" Keppler screamed.

Dan Murdoch shrugged. "All right, if that's the way you feel about it. But you're missing a real bargain."

He took his foot out of the door. Keppler tried to close it, but suddenly something was jabbed into his side. He had turned away from Paid Strang for a moment, and Paul was now poking a gun into his ribs.

The Nazi Vice-Consul's face grew mottled with rage.

Paul moved quickly out into the corridor. He took Dan Murdoch's arm. "Let's see those magazines of yours," he said. "Maybe I'll take a subscription."

"Why that's fine, mister." Murdoch smiled, and together they moved down the hall toward the elevator.

Keppler fingered the gun in his pocket. He remembered his orders from Albrecht to kill young Strang; but he also realized that in order to do it now, he must also shoot the magazine sales-man. To do that, here in a public corridor, would bring plenty of trouble—it would mean that he would not be free to keep his tryst with Albrecht for the big blow-off!

The elevator stopped at the floor. Paul Strang and Dan Murdoch got into it.

"Lucky fool!" Keppler muttered. "If that magazine salesman had not happened to come to the door, you would be dead by now!

He couldn't know that the "magazine salesman" had not come to the door by accident at all, but rather as the result of a beautifully timed plan.

CHAPTER 6
INFERNO!

A T SIX o'clock every night except Sunday, four thousand men left mammoth Lane Locomotive Works Plant, and four thousand others entered. The change of shifts was an inspiring thing to behold. Only a few months ago, the plant had been crawling along at one-fifth capacity, on a single shift. Now, under the spur of a driving faith in our own way of life and a deep-felt conviction that it must be defended at all costs, this great industrial plant was operating at two hundred percent its former capacity. New shops had been added, new assembly lines, new manpower—and a new spirit.

These skilled workers, coming in with their lunch boxes, wore the happy expressions of men who know they are earning a living and, at the same time, serving their country....

Kerrigan, Murdoch and Klaw stood with Paul Strang near one of the five employees' gates, watching the workers.

Each of them wore a badge, with his picture and a number on it. Ellen Lane had got them those badges, without which they wouldn't have been able to enter the plant. For months now, she had taken an active interest in the operation of the plant. The workmen loved her; their families swore by her, for she had visited many of them when they were sick.

Steve Klaw had braved the police hunt in the city, to go to a photographer's and have the pictures of himself, Kerrigan and Murdoch printed into the spaces on the badge. Thus, they were all armed with their passports into the Works.

"The way I figure it," Murdoch said, "this must be the place that Albrecht and Keppler are interested in. When the door was open, I got a quick look into the office. There was a telescope on the desk. And the window looked right out toward this plant."

"If you're right," Steve Klaw said, "it was a clever piece of work to send Paul up there. If you're wrong, we'll be wasting our time tonight."

"We might as well go in," said Johnny Kerrigan. "The whistle will be blowing in a minute. If anything's slated to happen, we'd better be inside."

The four of them joined the moving throng, and passed through the gate without being challenged.

Paul Strang looked a little worried. "I'm going over to the Executive Office. Ellen will be there. If anything breaks, I want to be near her."

"Right," said Stephen Klaw. "The program is to separate now, sort of snoop around. If nothing happens in an hour, we meet at this gate."

He glanced around. To the left were the proving grounds for the baby tanks; beyond them, the testing field for the heavy tanks. The baby tanks, under a new plan being formulated by the British, were to be used as a screen for the big monsters. These little ones could travel at sixty miles per hour, and the important secret of the Lane Locomotive Works was their hundred-ton tank which was geared in such proportion that it could travel at the same speed. It was the secret which Albrecht wanted so badly.

"You better take the proving grounds, Shrimp," Kerrigan said. "You took a course in tank maneuver. If there's anything screwy going on over there, you'll be able to smell it out."

"All right," said Steve. "And you better take the forge. Dan will take the Assembly Plant. Remember: Back here in an hour!"

STEPHEN KLAW moved out into the proving grounds, one of a hundred men. His keen eyes studied these others, then swept onto the field, where an experimental baby tank was waiting to be tested.

He was halfway across the grounds when he heard the shrill

whistle—three sharp blasts, then two. The sound cut across the field, stopping the men in their tracks. It was a new sound.

Almost at once, a great red streak of fire burst into life behind them, near the gate. It flamed across the yard, struck against the steel of the Administration Building. The hot flame seared the face of the building, swung down and slashed through the windows—at the workers inside!

At the same time, other flame-throwers burst into fiery brilliance in other parts of the plant. Screams came now from all sides.

Stephen Klaw cursed under his breath. Albrecht's men had struck without delay. How many of them there might be, he had no way of telling, but that they would be well organized, he was sure. Their plan would succeed, unless he and Kerrigan and Murdoch stopped it. Three men against an organized group of destruction!

All over the place now, the terrible *flammenwerfer* were hurling blazing death at the workers. Thousands of men and women were running about madly, in frenzied panic.

Steve caught sight of Murdoch and Kerrigan, together, their guns blazing in unison as they fought back a group of flame-throwers from a great milling throng of workers. Kerrigan and Murdoch weren't going to join him. They were going to stop right there and protect those defenseless men and women.

Steve groaned. They were throwing away their lives! They couldn't hope to hold those *flammenwerfer* off for more than a couple of minutes. When their guns were empty, they would go down....

Steve deliberately turned and ran in the opposite direction!

The men around him had dispersed, seeking shelter as best they could, and he had the field to himself. He covered it like a sprinter, heading straight for that baby tank in the proving grounds.

There was no one near it. He climbed up into the open turret, breathing a silent prayer that it was fully equipped and ready for an action test.

He slid in under the controls, and his practiced fingers found the starter button. He shoved it in, fed her gas, and the tank rumbled a quick response.

Steve Klaw breathed another prayer, one of fervent thanks, this time. The tank reacted to his every touch on the controls. He sent it hurtling across the field, toward where Kerrigan and Murdoch were fighting off the *flammenwerfer*. The machine bounced over a rough spot, jolting him hard, but he only grinned, and stepped up the speed. He pulled the trip of the manifold machine-gun on the front of the turret, and let go with a trial burst. The slugs sang across the field, high over the *flammenwerfer*.

Kerrigan and Murdoch saw him coming. They shouted to him.

The *flammenwerfer* saw the tank too, and turned their attention from the slaughter of defenseless men and women to a real battle. Steve, his eyes glittering with unholy pleasure, lowered the sights of the machine-gun, and sent a burst right into their midst. The hail of slugs from the quadruple-banked forward machine-guns mowed down the flame-throwers.

53

Steve headed straight for Johnny and Dan, yelling for them to climb aboard. The danger was far from over, for most of the flame-throwers were coming from other parts of the vast plant, in a mass attack on the single tank. At their head was the pudgy figure of *Doktor* Albrecht, with Keppler at his side.

Steve spied Ellen Lane and Paul Strang, off to the left, running toward them. Paul staggered as a bullet hit him.

Far to the right, Steve spied the source of that shot. Some of the Nazis had captured the guard tower near the gate. They were entrenched there with machine-guns and they were raking the yard.

Steve headed the tank toward Ellen, who was trying to support Paul Strang and run with him at the same time. Kerrigan and Murdoch reached them at the same time, and Steve swung the tank around in such a way as to shield Ellen and Paul from the machine-gun in the guard tower.

Dan Murdoch got hold of Paul, hauled him up, and dumped down inside the tank. Then he stood next to Steve, head and shoulders out of the turret, disdainful of the barrage from the guard tower. He swung the rear machine-guns to bear on the Nazis—just as the attack from the *flammenwerfer* broke against them.

THE FLAME-THROWERS were spread out in open array, under the direction of Albrecht and Keppler. From three sides at once, the hot fire concentrated on the tank.

Steve held the machine right where it was, for Kerrigan was trying to boost Ellen Lane inside. He couldn't get a hold on the smooth metal side, and Dan Murdoch swiftly ripped off his belt, fastened it around a strut, and let the other end hang.

"Grab it, Johnny!" he yelled, above the sounds of battle.

Kerrigan grinned. He had his arm around Ellen's waist. With his other hand he gripped the strap, and boosted himself up. As soon as he was on, Steve swung the tank around and headed right into the thick of the flame-throwers. Kerrigan dumped Ellen inside, alongside of Paul, and took his place at the port guns. Now, the three of them worked those machine-guns like men possessed. Kerrigan and Klaw turned their fire on the flame-throwers, while Murdoch concentrated on the guard tower.

Hot flame seared their faces, and bullets whipped a leaden hail around them. But the three grinning ghouls of destiny didn't heed the fire or the bullets. They rode down onto the flame-throwers without slackening speed....

All through the fight, Stephen Klaw kept his eye on Albrecht. At last, there were only a handful of the flame-throwers left. They had taken refuge in a corner at the angle where two buildings met. And now, as the tank headed toward them, they threw down their deadly weapon and raised their hands.

"*Kamerad!*" they shouted. Foremost among those who shouted surrender were Albrecht and Keppler.

Stephen Klaw growled. "Do we have to let those rats live?"

"I think not!" Dan Murdoch softly. He pointed at a mob of men—workers in the plant—who were sweeping down upon the Nazis.

Ten minutes later, Dan Murdoch said soberly, "Well, Albrecht and Keppler died quickly, anyway. If they had ever got back to Germany, they might have died the hard way, as penalty for failure."

Kerrigan, Murdoch and Klaw looked at each other solemnly. Then they looked at Ellen Lane, who was binding Paul's wound and whispering in his ear.

"H'mph!" said Kerrigan "Let's get out of here."

"Let's get a drink," said Dan Murdoch. "I need one."

THE SUICIDE SQUAD'S
PRIVATE WAR

CHAPTER 1
THE LITTLE GRAY OLD MAN

THIS HAPPENED on October First. At the time, Stephen Klaw had no reason to suspect the tremendous issues which were to be involved, or to guess at the nature of the thing which would take place two days later, on October Third. For that matter, Military Intelligence didn't guess it either; nor did any of those who were in a far better position to guess than was Stephen Klaw.

It all started with the note Carl Bishopp sent to the Washington office of the F.B.I. It read:

"I can tell you all about the Black Troop and the Little Gray Old Man. It's worth ten thousand dollars. If you want to do business, put an ad in the Times' Personals and say: Susan come home, the rent is paid. *Then on Monday night, have Stephen Klaw come to the Fantasy Bar on Broadway, any time from seven o'clock on. Let him bring half the money. After you check my information, you can pay me the other half. I am picking Klaw because I know him, and I won't have much time to look for someone I do not know. I am in hiding now, and the chances are that I'll be spotted by the Black Troop, so be sure that Klaw is there. If you put the ad in the paper, I*

He twisted around on top of Von Reichenstein and let him have one full in the face.

*will take it that you agree not to arrest me or detain me in any way.
On my part, I promise to give Klaw definite information about the
Little Gray Old Man. You can trust me. I have done business with
you before.*

Carl Bishopp"

Stephen Klaw didn't like to do business with informers.
However, in this instance, he had no choice but to accept the
assignment.

Kerrigan and Murdoch, who said goodbye to him when
he boarded the plane at Washington, kidded him about the
"dangerous" job he was undertaking.

"Look out for the Little Gray Old Man," Murdoch taunted.
"He may slap you on the wrist."

Johnny Kerrigan added his two cents' worth. "If anybody talks
rough to you in New York, Shrimp, tell 'em you'll get your two
big partners after them."

"Nuts to you both!" Steve said sourly.

Had Murdoch and Kerrigan known how dangerous that job
would turn out to be, or just how deadly the Little Gray Old
Man could be, wild horses couldn't have kept them off that
plane.

Of the Black Troop there had been many rumors; disjointed,
fragmentary reports. It was known that the Black Troop was the
vast, really secret Axis spy organization which operated throughout the world. No one had heard of it until recently, for they
had covered up with consummate cleverness. Periodically, the
activities of other Nazi and Fascist organizations were exposed,

but those were virtually harmless groups, in comparison to the Black Troop.

Yet, this was the first hint about the Little Gray Old Man. Who or what he was, neither the F.B.I., nor Military Intelligence, nor even the British Intelligence knew.

If they had known, they might have sent more than one man to contact Carl Bishopp....

AT TWENTY minutes after eight on that designated Monday evening, Stephen Klaw had been in the Fantasy Bar for exactly one hour and fifteen minutes; and nothing had happened yet.

But at twenty-one minutes past eight, Carl Bishopp walked in.

Steve saw him in the mirror, recognizing him instantly. Five years ago, Bishopp had furnished information which had enabled him—together with Kerrigan and Murdoch—to capture a band of extortionists.

Bishopp was a tall man, with a wide mouth and a pair of black eyes which seemed to touch everywhere at once. But tonight, as Steve glimpsed him coming through the door of the Fantasy Bar, the stool pigeon's eyes were unnaturally sharp, and his face was so white it looked as if it had been bleached. There was a nervous tremor to his lower lip; and though he walked very erect, it seemed as if he were afraid he would fall over.

Bishopp's left hand was dug deeply into his pocket, his right held something which bulged underneath his coat.

He spotted Stephen Klaw at the bar, and came directly toward him, walking like a drunk who is desperately trying to follow a straight line. He reached Steve's side, took his left hand out of his pocket to grasp the bar. He kept his right hand under his coat.

"Klaw," he said.

The man's voice was no more than a smothered gasp.

"Hello," said Steve. "What's the matter with you?"

Bishopp's lips trembled. "Did you bring the money, Klaw?"

"I have it in my pocket."

"Fine!" Bishop smiled a twisted, bitter smile. "Give it away. Give it to charity. Because it's no good—to me any—more."

He brought his left into sight, letting his coat fall open. Steve saw then what was underneath: A knife!

Only the handle was showing. The rest of it was driven into Bishopp's body. He had been holding it tightly against himself, so that the handle guard prevented excessive bleeding.

Bishopp made no attempt to pull the knife out. He put his left hand on the bar, so that both hands were supporting him now.

"They got me!" he gasped, with that crooked, bitter smile still on his lips. "Just around the corner. I should have known—couldn't outsmart—the Little Gray Old—Man. Money's no good to—me now—"

A fleck of crimson appeared at the corner of his mouth. His knees buckled and he slipped to the floor.

Steve caught him, eased him down on his side.

"Bishopp! You're dying!"

"I know—"

"What were you going to tell me about the Black Troop?

Speak up, man. It's the last thing you'll do on this earth. Make it a *good* thing!"

Bishopp's sharp, feverish eyes were closing as he gasped for breath. But that bitter smile was still hovering on his lips.

"No money—in it—now. Maybe I'm a stoolie—no good. But I'm—an American. Get the Black Troop—quick. Only forty-eight hours to go. Look out for the—Little Gray Old Man. He's—poison. And look out for the woman with the ash-blonde hair. Big blow-off is set—for Friday at—San Felix...."

That was all.

Stephen Klaw lowered Bishopp's head to the floor, and stood up. Carl Bishopp was dead.

THE MUSIC at the rear had stopped, and everybody in the place had come crowding around. They bombarded Steve with questions.

A policeman pushed his way through the crowd.

"Who is he?" he barked at Steve, after he had satisfied himself that Bishopp was dead.

Steve shrugged. "I never saw him before in my life," he lied.

Someone in the crowd shouted, "He came right over to you. I saw him!"

"Can I help it?" Steve demanded innocently.

"What was he telling you while you were holding him?" the heckler insisted truculently.

Steve's eyes flickered momentarily. "He was delirious. He was reciting poetry."

"Poetry?" the cop repeated incredulously.

Stephen Klaw's glance slid around the crowd. He spotted

several men at the fringe—men who had not been in the place before. Could they be Bishopp's killers, come in to make sure he had died quickly, without talking?

"What kind of poetry?" The cop was insistent now.

"It was a song," Steve said. "The guy was singing *The Old Gray Mare.* That's what it sounded like. Only he called it *The Little Old Gray Mare.*"

He saw a man at the back of the crowd smile suddenly, as if he were enjoying a private joke. Then the fellow turned and hurried out.

Steve started to follow, but the cop put a heavy hand on his arm.

"Now wait, mister," the policeman said with heavy sarcasm. "Don't you think the police are entitled to just a little statement? Couldn't you spare us a couple of minutes till the sergeant gets here?"

"I'll be right back," Steve told him. "I just saw a friend of mine—"

"Is that so? Now listen here, you—"

"It's perfectly all right, officer," Steve said. "Here's my name and address. You can always get me if you need me."

He took out his Federal Bureau of Investigation identification card case, opened it, making sure that no one in the crowd could see what it was.

The policeman glanced at it; he whistled.

"Quiet!" Steve whispered.

"Go ahead, buddy," said the cop. "I didn't know you were *the*

Mr. Brown!" He winked at Steve, no doubt believing himself very clever.

Steve winked back, and hurried out of the Fantasy Bar.

The man he had seen was already turning the far corner. Steve hurried after him, and reached the corner in time to see the man disappear into a taxi which roared down a side street. He noted the number of the cab; he was about to take out a pencil and jot it down when he became aware of motion at his elbow.

He whirled, his eyes narrowing involuntarily, to shade the light of battle in them.

A little, wrinkled old man stood beside him.

HE WAS a neat little old man, with gray hair straggling out from under a gray felt hat. He was cleanly shaven, but badly in need of a haircut. His shirt was clean and white, although the collar was frayed. He wore a black bow tie, and he had a black wire around his neck. It ran to a hearing device behind his right ear. His gray suit was old, but neatly pressed. He was carrying a bunch of pencils in one hand.

He looked up at Stephen Klaw, smiling, his blue eyes twinkling in a friendly manner.

"Excuse me, young man," he said. "Would you care to buy a pencil?"

"Sure," said Steve. He took one of the pencils, and wrote down the number of the taxicab in his notebook. He gave the old man a quarter.

"What's your name, dad?" he asked.

"Ricks," said the old man. "They call me Pappy Ricks around

here." He fumbled around in his pocket for change of the quarter.

"Keep it," Steve said.

"Thanks, young man." The old man put the quarter in his pocket. He pressed four more pencils into Steve's hand. "I don't take charity, young man. I'm in the pencil business."

Stephen Klaw studied the wrinkled face, and in his mind he kept hearing Bishopp's dying words: *Look out for the Little Gray Old Man. He's—poison.*

"I see you just come out of the Fantasy Bar," the gray old man commented. "Something happened in there, eh?"

Steve said, "Carl Bishopp died in there."

He watched the old man's eyes, but couldn't note any reaction.

"Carl Bishopp?" the old man repeated. "Is he someone important?"

"Very important," Steve told him.

The old man's eyes were blue and innocent. "That's funny. I've been on Broadway for many years—I know all the important people along the Main Stem, even if only by their pictures. I never heard of Carl Bishopp." He shrugged. "How did he die?"

Steve was in a spot, and knew it. He couldn't figure this old man at all. Either he was just an innocent pencil vendor, or he was a dangerous spymaster who had just brought about the death of Carl Bishopp, and was now doing a beautiful bit of acting. Klaw couldn't go around arresting every little old man he saw, merely on the strength of a dead stool-pigeon's statement that the Little Gray Old Man was the head of the Black Troop.

Steve tried a shot in the dark. "*You* ought to know how he died," he said.

"*I?*" The old man's eyes were questioning now. "Why should *I* know?"

"He had one of your pencils in his hand when he came in," Steve said, inventing that last detail conveniently.

The old man shook his head. "Couldn't be. You're the first one this evening who has bought a pencil."

"I'll tell you, Pop," Steve said, deciding to take the plunge. "Bishopp was stabbed by a member of the Black Troop, at the order of the Little Gray Old Man. There's a good chance that's you." He opened his identification card case and showed it to the other. "I'm a Federal Officer. I have no authority to arrest you on a charge of suspicion of murder, but I can turn you over to the local authorities. Will you come back to the Fantasy Bar with me?"

The old man looked absolutely bewildered. "I think you're crazy, young man. You don't look more than a kid just out of college. That's what's wrong nowadays. They give kids like you too much authority. How could you ever believe I killed anyone?"

His voice had risen by degrees as he spoke, so that now he was almost shouting. Passing people stopped to look. The cop who had let Steve out of the Fantasy Bar came down toward them. He had been busy shooing people away from the front of the place, and the old man's voice had carried to him quite easily.

"What's up now?" the policeman demanded truculently.

Steve nodded toward the little old man. "I want you to arrest this man, officer, on a charge of suspicion of murder."

Just then, a heavy-set man pushed through the crowd. The man was impeccably dressed, in evening clothes. His face was ruddy, and he sported a small, carefully-trimmed moustache.

He was strangely and violently indignant. "I'm Mark Cronin, the lawyer!" he said, as if everyone should know him. Steve *had* heard of him, all right. Mark Cronin was the city's foremost criminal lawyer. He was said to charge a thousand dollars for each day he spent in court.

"Look here," Cronin swept on, authoritatively, glaring at Steve. "I heard what you just said. It's ridiculous to accuse Pappy Ricks of murder—of anything. He wouldn't harm a fly. Why, I've known him for years. He's the most harmless man on Broadway. I've bought a pencil from him every night, right here on this corner, for more than fifteen years!"

STEPHEN KLAW felt the hostile stares which were directed against him. The little old man looked more helpless and harmless than ever as he turned his innocent blue eyes on the lawyer.

"Thank you, Mr. Cronin," he said. "Thank you again. But you mustn't blame this young G-man. He's just a kid—and no doubt apt to make mistakes. Let's forget about the whole thing—"

"I'm sorry," Steve said, "but I must insist on this arrest."

The cop scratched his head, looking appraisingly at Stephen Klaw. It was true that Steve didn't seem to be more than a kid just out of college; his slim and wiry build was deceptive. No one, glancing at him casually, would ever have suspected that he was one of the three most feared fighting men on the rolls of the F.B.I.

"Better think it over, Klaw," the cop said. "Pappy Ricks is an old stand-by on Broadway. I've known him for years. He was here before I ever started on the beat. Have you got anything definite on him?"

"Just a hunch," Steve answered.

"Aha!" shouted Mark Cronin, the criminal lawyer. "Just a hunch, eh? Since when do we arrest people on hunches in this country?" He put a hand on the old man's shoulder. "Let him arrest you, Pappy. Then you can sue him and the F.B.I. for a million dollars damages. I'll handle the case gratis!"

"Skip it!" Steve said suddenly. "Let's forget about the whole incident. What say, Pappy? Let's shake and make up!"

He extended his hand in a sudden, friendly gesture.

Pappy Ricks smiled. "Gladly, young man!" He accepted Steve's proffered hand, his grip surprisingly strong for such a frail-looking old man. The swift gleam of triumph in his innocent blue eyes was swiftly subdued.

For just an instant, the blue eyes of the old man met the cold gray ones of Stephen Klaw, and all pretense, all sham dropped away. There was pure hate in Pappy Ricks' blue eyes, and a challenge, or a promise of future conflict.

Whatever the crowd thought of this strange scene, only the two men who gripped palms knew each other's thoughts. They were two adversaries who had unmasked each other, and each had gained a point. The old man had learned that Klaw was a G-man; he knew, probably, that Klaw had come to meet Bishopp. Steve, on the other hand, was certain that this was the Little Gray Old Man, the leader of the Black Troop; but he was equally certain that he could get nowhere by forcing an arrest. This Little Gray Old Man was no average criminal. Nothing would be found on him if he were taken to headquarters. He was, no doubt, clever enough to have created for himself this character of old Pappy Ricks, and to have built it up to the point where it could not be easily broken through.

No, it would take more than the death of a man like Bishopp to force the Little Gray Old Man into the open.

But now the battle was begun, and each knew where the other stood. That handshake had not been unlike the handshake of two prizefighters in the ring, who in a moment would be slugging each other.

Stephen Klaw let go of that old man's hand and nodded good-night.

Twenty minutes later, he was on the long distance phone to Washington, talking to his Chief, the Director of the F.B.I.

Tersely, he reported what had happened. "So they closed Bishopp's mouth," he concluded. "But Bishopp had the info, all right—he put me on to the Little Gray Old Man. That old bird is the leader of the Black Troop—I'll take an oath on it. But we can't prove it in court."

"We'll shadow him," said the Chief. "I'll put some of the men from the New York office on it—and on Mark Cronin, too, just to make sure."

"What about this San Felix tip that Bishopp gave me? Isn't there going to be a practice blackout in San Felix Friday?"

"Yes. And we have something else on it here. We got an anonymous note warning us to watch for trouble during the San Felix blackout. We're tracing a lead on that note. It was mailed from Saint Louis. I've already sent Kerrigan and Murdoch there, and I want you to take a plane and meet them there tomorrow."

"But what about this end? Couldn't I work here in New York? I'd like to—"

"Never mind what you'd like!" the Chief told him sharply. "I want you in Saint Louis. You're known to the Black Troop now, and all you'll do is get yourself killed if you stay in New York. Saint Louis it is. That's orders."

Steve Klaw grumbled a little, but he knew he'd have to obey.

And that is why Kerrigan, Murdoch and Klaw were neither in San Felix nor in New York on Friday, when that other thing took place in San Felix.

CHAPTER 2
"FIND LORD CHESTER!"

AT NINE o'clock Friday evening, October 3rd, a siren screamed, and every light in the city of San Felix went out.

Traffic stopped; headlights blinked out; cigarettes were snuffed. Air-raid wardens took over.

The city's streets were not deserted. On the contrary, they were filled with countless people, eager-eyed men, women and children who were frankly pleased with this intriguing incident. Everybody had turned out tonight to witness the first large-scale practice air-raid and blackout in the United States.

A buzzing hum of conversation ran up and down Main Street, as the volunteer air-raid wardens patrolled the Avenue, intoning their repeated warning: *"Show no lights, please. Show no lights, please!"*

Thousands of heads craned toward the south, and at last someone shouted, "There they are! See those bombers!"

At the same time, the air was filled with the throbbing of many motors, and against the purple sky were outlined the silhouettes of the great, stately Boeings and Consolidateds which were winging their way on schedule from the south—from which direction an enemy attack might logically be attempted.

Anti-aircraft batteries opened up on the outer edges of the city. Competent observers, stationed on roof tops, would be able to tell which of the planes were theoretically shot down.

The objective of the "attacking" planes was assumed to be the water works, the gas and electric plants, and the railroad station. Any planes which succeeded in evading the anti-aircraft fire would fly over the designated objectives; the bombardier, instead of dropping a bomb, would click the shutter of an infra-red camera, after releasing a flare. Thus, he would have photographic proof that he had scored a theoretical "hit."

The residents of San Felix were enjoying the show immensely.

"See that plane, Momma!" Gus Kromlech stood at the corner of Main and Fourth, with his wife and their two children. Gus was a Czechoslovakian who had been in America for twenty-eight years now; he had married and raised a family here, working all his life in the great San Felix aluminum plant.

"That plane, Momma!" he pointed directly overhead. "It's right over us. Thank God this is not Prague. Thank God that is not a German bomber!"

As he spoke, a long, cigar-shaped object dropped from the underside of the plane above.

Gus Kromlech was standing there, with his finger in the air, his mouth open but voicing no sound. And that is the way he died—he and Momma and their two children, and hundreds of people all around them....

The cigar-shaped object struck the earth a few feet away; it detonated in a terrible ground-shattering explosion which destroyed everything within the radius of a hundred yards.

Simultaneously, other bombs came screaming down, from other planes, to spread death and destruction throughout the city. Bombs landed on the water works, on the gas and electric works.

The crowd that had come out to enjoy the thrill of mock warfare had no chance to flee. The streets were strewn with corpses....

In the midst of the panic which filled the blacked-out city, men appeared from cellars and darkened doorways. They were grim men, each wearing a black armband, each provided with an automatic pistol or a carbine. They moved through the streets with callous disregard for the wounded, and headed for the Royal Hotel.

Here no bombs had fallen. Several official cars were parked before the entrance of the hotel, and a platoon of Marines stood on guard at the door.

They were only a handful, those Marines, but when they saw the grim, advancing horde of attackers, their officer barked an order, and they opened fire.

But they were overwhelmed by the numbers of those men with the black armbands, who swept over their dead bodies into the hotel. Swiftly, those men took possession of the lobby by ruthless use of carbine and pistol. They produced flashlights, and moving with the precision of a well-trained army thoroughly drilled in each step they went through the upper floors of the hotel. A small compact group took the stairs to the roof after the elevators had been put out of commission.

ON THE roof-top, they seemed to know exactly what they would find. Five men were standing there, close to the parapet, staring tensely out over the city. Two of these men wore army uniform; three were in civilian clothes. Of the three civilians, only one did not move when the horde of attackers reached upon the roof. He was a tall man, in formal attire; he wore a monocle which complemented well his distinctly British moustache.

The two officers and the two other civilians snatched at revolvers.

It was their last animate act. A well-directed burst from the attackers cut down the four men before they could use their weapons. The tall Britisher was left standing alone, close to the edge of the roof.

Calmly, he faced the attackers. Deliberately, he placed one foot on the parapet.

The leader of the attacking horde called sharply, "Don't move, Lord Chester! If you attempt to jump, I shall shoot you in the knee-cap. You will still be our prisoner, with the added disadvantage of a broken leg!"

The leader was a, little old man, with gray hair, a wrinkled face and light blue eyes. But somehow, he no longer resembled the little old man whom Stephen Klaw had met in New York two days ago. Perhaps it was because he was now wearing a gray military raincoat instead of his threadbare suit; or perhaps it was because the heavy, businesslike Luger in his gray-gloved hand gave him an appearance of power. His posture was soldierly. His blue eyes were no longer innocent and helpless; they gleamed with a new, venomous force which had not been there before, except for the moment when he and Stephen Klaw had locked grips and glances.

Lord Chester, who had never seen the man before, must have realized that here was no petty leader of a crowd of ruffians. This was a man whose cold grim menace spoke of a keen intellect, a sharp intelligence.

But Lord Chester knew only too well the danger of being taken prisoner. He threw one leg over the parapet.

"The devil with you!" he exclaimed, and attempted to leap.

These men of the Black Troop had been prepared for every and any emergency. From somewhere in that group of men who wore black armbands came the *whirr* of a slingshot. A round leaden pellet whizzed through the air, struck Lord Chester along the side of the head. The tall Britisher gasped and swayed dizzily, there at the edge of the roof. And in that moment, the men of the Black Troop seized him.

Lord Chester swayed on his feet, in the grip of his captors, and faced the Little Gray Old Man. The latter watched him out of those deadly blue eyes, as a cobra might eye a luckless bird.

"What do you say now, Lord Chester?"

Even in his helpless position, the Britisher exhibited that cool dignity which has always infuriated the enemies of England.

"Go to the devil. I know why you are doing this. You and your beastly Black Troop have staged this whole raid solely for the purpose of capturing me. You think that I will talk."

The Little Gray Old Man nodded. "Assuredly, Lord Chester. I'm certain you will talk."

"Then you're mistaken. I'd die first."

"You might want to die, Lord Chester. You might even beg to die. But I promise you that you'll talk. Once we have you out of this accursed country, there will be plenty of time for us to deal with you at our leisure. I've never yet failed to make a man talk, my dear Lord Chester!"

He turned his flashlight on his wrist watch. It was twelve minutes after nine.

"Bring the prisoner along," he ordered curtly, speaking in German. "We are exactly on schedule. The stolen Army trucks will be waiting for us below."

WHEN KERRIGAN, Murdoch and Klaw arrived in San Felix at twenty minutes past midnight, the bombed city was busy digging itself out of the ruins. The population moved about in a daze. Not one person in fifty thousand knew about what had happened at the Royal Hotel.

The city was under martial law. The National Guard had moved in, supported by a motorized unit from a nearby training camp. Every exit from the city was patrolled; no one was permitted in the streets without a pass. Kerrigan, Murdoch and Klaw were whisked through the littered streets in an F.B.I. car.

The Director of the Federal Bureau of Investigation was waiting for them in a room on the top floor of the Royal Hotel. The top floor was a beehive of excitement. The Secretary of State was there in another room, as well as the British Ambassador, and a hundred other officials of the Army, the Air Force, Military Intelligence and the Diplomatic Service. But in the room where the Director of the F.B.I. interviewed his three hellions of the Suicide Squad, there was no one else present.

The Director's face was grim his eyes bleak and hard, as he looked at Stephen Klaw. "Well, Bishopp knew what he was talking about: The big blow-on at San Felix! It certainly broke big!"

He was pacing up and down as be talked. Then be stopped abruptly and faced them. "I'm going to give you the inside dope. There are only three other people who are in the know, the Secretary of State, the British Ambassador—and the President! From what we've been able to learn, there were ninety-six of our bombers taking part in the practice air-raid. They took off from six different fields, in squadrons, and met at a point twenty miles south of San Felix, then headed over the city."

The Director paused, his lips tight. "But somewhere along the line, in the darkness, those ninety-six bombers were joined by six others. *And those six carried real bombs!*"

Kerrigan, Murdoch and Klaw glanced at each other. But none of them said a word. They waited for their Chief to go on.

"All the time that we've been fighting sabotage and Fifth Column activity in this country, that Little Gray Old Man and his Black Troop have been organizing unmolested. Imagine the vast resources that Black Troop must possess, to have established a secret airport somewhere, and provided bombing planes; to have acquired the inside information of our plans. And they've succeeded, far better than you may suspect. In fact, they've practically dealt us a knockout blow—unless you three men work fast."

Stephen Klaw frowned. "I don't get it, Chief. You say they've dealt us a death blow. It looked pretty bad from the air, as we flew in. The water works and the power plants have been wrecked, and the steel factories on the edge of town have been practically destroyed. But that's not what I call a death blow—"

"Of course not!" exclaimed the Director. "Anybody can see that the damage is bad, but that, after all, this is only one town. It could be wiped off the map without making any appreciable difference in our total defense effort. The death blow I refer to is something else again—something that only three other people know about as yet."

He began to walk again, then stopped just as suddenly. "You've all heard of Lord Chester Breedsley?"

"Sure," said Johnny Kerrigan in his big, booming voice. "He's the British Minister without Portfolio. He's in this country on a secret mission. He was scheduled to leave tomorrow morning on a British battle cruiser from Tampa, Florida."

"Exactly. Lord Chester was here to arrange the final steps in the coördination between our Pacific Battle Fleet and the British Expeditionary Force in Malaysia. He was given the details of the disposition and numbers of our Battle Fleet, and of our forces in the Far East. That information was so dangerous that he didn't dare put it on paper. He was carrying it back to England in his head. And he intended to leave on a battle cruiser, mind you, not a destroyer."

"So?" Dan Murdoch asked tensely, his dark, handsome face revealing that he had already guessed the answer, as had his two partners.

"So Lord Chester was here, on the roof of the Royal Hotel, watching the sham air-raid. His presence was absolutely secret— or so we thought. He was guarded by a detail of marines, two army intelligence officers, and two of our own boys, Brady and Katz."

Stephen Klaw's lips thinned as he recalled the bodies he had seen in the hotel lobby.

The Director nodded bitterly. "Brady and Katz are dead. So are the two Intelligence Officers. So are the Marines. But *we haven't found the body of Lord Chester!*"

"Then he was captured!" Dan Murdoch exclaimed.

"God help him!" said Johnny Kerrigan.

"God help *us!*" corrected the Chief. "If Lord Chester's captors once succeed in spiriting him out of the country to a place where they can work on him, they'll surely make him talk. No matter how brave or determined he may be, he's sure to break down under the methods those beasts will use. Oh, it will be subtle torture, all right, calculated to wreck his nervous system; maybe they'll administer drugs. But he'll talk…."

"And if he talks?" Johnny Kerrigan asked softly.

The Chief uttered a harsh laugh. "We have stuck our chin out in the Pacific, and in the Far East, too. Our Battle Fleet is out on a limb, without proper aerial support. We need three weeks more at least to consolidate our position. That's a secret. But you know how the pot is boiling in the Far East. If the Axis gets wind of the situation, they'll strike without delay. So far, the only thing that's been holding them has been their uncertainty of our Fleet disposition. Lord Chester can tell them all that."

STEPHEN KLAW spoke for the three of them. "We understand, all right. All we're supposed to do is find Lord Chester Breedsley, and take him away from the big bad boys who've got him. You tell us where he is, and we'll go get him."

"Shut up," said the Director. "I bet you three hellions would joke at your own funeral. But I do have a lead for you."

From his portfolio he extracted an envelope. From the envelope he took a bit of brown wrapping paper, about three inches by six, with ragged edges, which indicated that it had been hurriedly ripped from a larger piece. Upon it was a typewritten message:

> *"FBI—Look out for trouble at the San Felix blackout Friday. The Little Gray Old Man is behind it all. I know what I'm talking about.*
> *A Friend"*

The envelope had an airmail stamp and was postmarked from Saint Louis. It was the note which the Chief had mentioned when he had talked with Steve over the long-distance telephone.

"Dan and Johnny saw this before they left for Saint Louis," the Chief said. "Turn it over."

Steve turned the bit of wrapping paper over. His eyes

narrowed as he noted a fragment of a typed series of numbers: J2654—

He looked up at the Director, who nodded. "The one who wrote this note thought he was clever. He wanted very badly to remain anonymous, and warn us at the same time. So he mailed it from Saint Louis, after having written it in New York. We traced it. Those figures are part of the subscriber's serial number, stenciled on the wrapper of a magazine by an addressing machine.

"We went to work on it at once, contacted every periodical in the country. We found that it came from the wrapper of the Lawyer's Monthly, and the serial number belongs to one of their subscribers—Mark Cronin!"

Dan Murdoch whistled. He looked at Steve. "Cronin's the guy who put up the yap about your arresting the Little Gray Old Man."

Steve nodded. "But Cronin never wrote this. I'm sure of that. He's too smart. If he'd wanted to warn us, he'd have done it differently."

"You're quite right," said the Chief. "We sent Hillary, in New York, to check on Cronin's office. Cronin was out, but he talked to the girl, and she let him examine the typewriters in the office. This note was typed on the portable machine in Cronin's private office. And the only person in there yesterday who was left alone long enough, and who had the opportunity to do it, was a client of Cronin's—Lefty Lacosta."

"The guy who came out of Alcatraz last year!" Johnny Kerrigan frowned. "He's supposed to have a million bucks cached away."

Stephen Klaw said suddenly, "Carl Bishopp wanted to squeal to us, and the Black Troop knocked him off. Now Lefty Lacosta tries to warn us. It's dollars to doughnuts that the Little Gray Old Man will try to get him, too. Our job is to find where they've got Lord Chester, and to find it fast. We haven't got the ghost of a clue to go on. We can't comb the whole United States. But, if Johnny and Dan and I go to New York, maybe the Black Troop will show their hand with Lacosta, and that'll give us a chance—"

"That's what I'm hoping!" the Chief said. "Lacosta is being shadowed in New York, right now. Nothing will be done till you three get there. Then—well, you've got to start thing rolling, fast. Find Lord Chester inside of twenty-four hours, or I'm sure it'll be too late, because they'll have him spirited out of the country. You have either got to make Lacosta tell you everything he knows, or else you've got to do something drastic enough to bring the Black Troop and the Little Gray Old Man out in the open. Work on Lacosta; work on Cronin. Do anything you like. I give you an absolutely free hand, full authority, and no questions asked. *But find Lord Chester!*"

"Right, sir!" the three G-men exclaimed in unison.

"There's one thing more," the Chief said. He went over to the connecting door which led to the next room. "The British Ambassador is here, with his niece, Patricia Gilpin, who acts as his secretary. She came from New Zealand recently, and she's been helping out by taking the place of an able-bodied man. He wants you to take her along to New York. She didn't know about Lord Chester's disappearance. The ambassador has been telling her about it in the next room, while I've been talking here with you. You're to work with her. She'll provide your liaison with the British Consulate in New York, and with the British Secret Service, in case you should need them—"

"Now look, Chief," Johnny Kerrigan interrupted. "Isn't it bad enough you give us a nut like this to crack—without saddling us with a dame?"

The Director shrugged. "I'm sorry, Johnny. But it's orders. The ambassador has a reason for sending her along. You'll have to grin and bear it." He opened the connecting door.

The British Ambassador entered, with Patricia Gilpin on his arm.

JOHNNY KERRIGAN blinked twice when he saw her. She was tall, with ash-blonde hair, and beauty enough to take any man's breath away. It was hard to tell just how old she was. Anywhere from twenty-eight to thirty-five might have been a good guess. It was easy to see, from the capable and authoritative manner in which she carried herself, that she would make an efficient secretary for a diplomat.

But Stephen Klaw was not thinking of that. Through his head ran Carl Bishopp's dying words: *"Look out for the Little Gray Old Man. He's poison. And look out for the woman with the ash-blonde hair!"*

It was fantastic. This was the ambassador's niece—she couldn't be the woman Bishopp meant. Such a thing was incredible, beyond the bounds of reason. There was nothing to go on—

yet.... There had been less to go on when Steve wanted to arrest that little old man in Times Square. It was just as fantastic to have thought that the little old pencil vendor was the head of a vast and vicious spy-ring.

Watching the blonde girl, Steve saw that she had the bearing, the attitude, the manners of speech which would tend to prove that she was a British aristocrat's niece, recently arrived from New Zealand. But was she that—or a consummate actress?

She spared only a single glance apiece for Kerrigan and Murdoch, but she studied Stephen Klaw more carefully. Then she turned to the Director of the F.B.I.

Her voice was soft, almost purring, but it held a note of protest.

"Uncle has just told me of the terrible thing that has happened to Lord Chester. It—it's fantastic. I can hardly believe that you are sending only three men. In New Zealand, they would assign every policeman in the Dominion!"

Stephen Klaw turned away with a look of disgust. Johnny Kerrigan made a wry face, and Dan Murdoch just grinned.

The ambassador patted the girl on the shoulder. "Now, my dear, don't let your emotions get the better of you. I'm sure the Director here knows how to handle such matters. And I am told that these three gentlemen—Messrs. Kerrigan, Murdoch and Klaw—are the best in the country. They're the famous Suicide Squad."

Patricia Gilpin's eyes went wide. She turned a searching scrutiny upon the three G-men. "My word! I've heard of you— In the Auckland papers they always write you up." She grinned apologetically. "I hope I didn't seem rude."

"Skip it," Steve Klaw said.

The Director coughed diplomatically. "You have something to say to these men before they leave, Mr. Ambassador?"

"Yes, yes." The ambassador seemed ill-at-ease as he fumbled for words. "Your Director has no doubt told you how much Lord Chester's disappearance means to the safety of both our countries. You know what we stand to lose if his captors force him to talk."

Steve nodded. "We understand."

"Well—er—you are naturally going to try to rescue him. Should you locate the place where he is being held, you will, of course, make every effort to liberate him."

"Naturally," said Steve, puzzled.

"But suppose," the ambassador went on, rather haltingly, "just suppose that when you find Lord Chester, the—ah—circumstances are such that you will find rescue impossible. What then?"

Steve Klaw's eyes narrowed. "There'd probably be some fireworks, I guess."

"I'm sure there would. From what I have heard of your exploits in the past, you would probably throw away your lives in a futile attempt, even if you were sure rescue was impossible. They say that the Suicide Squad keeps going around looking for Death, but that Death is shy of them."

Steve looked impatient; Dan and Johnny looked annoyed.

The ambassador took a deep breath. "If you should encounter

such a situation—where rescue is impossible—there is something you must do; a thing which will be as distasteful to you as it is for me to order. Can you guess what it is?"

There was a long silence. Steve threw a side glance at Dan and Johnny, who nodded almost imperceptibly. He turned back to the ambassador.

"We can guess," he said softly. "If we can't rescue Lord Chester, *you want us to kill him!*"

There was sweat on the ambassador's brow. "You put it very brutally, Mr. Klaw."

"It's a brutal thing."

"Yes, it is a brutal thing to ask. Yet I'm sure Lord Chester would want it that way."

There was sympathy in Stephen Klaw's eyes. "Leave it to us," he said. "We'll use our best judgment."

Then he turned to his partners. "I guess we can go now."

"Wait," Patricia Gilpin said. "Did you forget me? I'm going with you!"

CHAPTER 3
"SEE YOU IN HELL!"

IN ADDITION to the million dollars which he was supposed to have tucked away somewhere in cash, Lefty Lacosta owned considerable real estate in Manhattan. One of those pieces of property was the Manx Hotel, just off Times Square. It was here that he had come, after his release from

Alcatraz. To all intents and purposes he was now a respectable hotel proprietor.

It was to the Manx Hotel that Kerrigan and Klaw went, after depositing Patricia Gilpin at the British Consulate. The trip by chartered plane had taken five hours to LaGuardia Airport, and twenty minutes by cab to Manhattan, so that they had arrived at the British Consulate at six o'clock in the morning.

Even at that ungodly hour, there was plenty of activity at the Consulate. The entire staff had been routed out of bed, and messengers were hurrying in and out of the building on Fifth Avenue.

Patricia Gilpin insisted on their coming upstairs to meet the Consul General and the New York head of the British Intelligence Service. This would have meant a loss of time, and there wasn't much of it to spare.

The plane's radio had kept them informed of the movements of Lefty Lacosta. He had returned to the Manx Hotel about two o'clock in the morning, and Hillary and West—two F.B.I. men from the New York Field Office—were covering the place, waiting for the Suicide! Squad to take over.

So Dan Murdoch had been delegated to go upstairs with Patricia Gilpin, while Steve and Johnny went on to the Manx Hotel.

The Times Square area never comes alive before ten o'clock in the morning. There was very little doing on the side street where the Manx was located. There were a couple of trucks being unloaded of vegetables at nearby restaurants along the block; a solitary milkman wrestled with a milk can at the service door of the hotel. Down at the far corner, Kerrigan and Klaw saw a policeman ringing in at his call box.

The morning was dreary, with no sun at all. A few drops of rain had begun to fall.

Johnny Kerrigan paid off the cab driver. He and Steve turned in to the hotel. Almost at once, they spotted the figure of Joe Hillary, one of the two New York G-men who were shadowing Lacosta.

Hillary was in the lobby pretending to read a newspaper, while sitting in such a position that he commanded a view of both the front and back entrances of the hotel.

The lobby was pretty busy for six o'clock in the morning. There were two men at the clerk's desk, apparently absorbed in the intricacies of a railroad timetable. Another man was idly smoking a cigar near the rear door, and two more were loitering at the cigar counter, which hadn't yet opened.

Hillary put down his paper when he saw Kerrigan and Klaw. He got up, came over toward them with a great show of cordiality.

"Why, hello, Mr. Spiegel, Mr. Walsh!" His voice was loud enough for everybody in the lobby to hear. "I been waiting for you an hour already, to show you my samples. Believe me, I got the best line of knitted socks in the city."

He had reached them now, and he gripped Steve's hand heartily, giving a very good imitation of a high-pressure salesman greeting a couple of out-of-town buyers.

But immediately he lowered his voice to a whisper. "There's stuff brewing here, Klaw," he said swiftly. "West is holed up in a broom closet on the tenth floor, opposite the door of Lacosta's room. I've been down here most of the night. See all these birds hanging around the lobby? They just began to drift in. Looks like trouble. I don't think we're fooling them much."

"Then let's forget this business about samples!" Steve Klaw snapped. "I like to come out in the open. What say, Johnny?"

"Me, too!" growled Kerrigan. "If these birds belong to the Black Troop, I say let's see what they're made of!"

Hillary shrugged. "It's your job, boys. Handle it any way you like."

Steve smiled. "We'll clear you first, anyway. You can stay on the sidelines."

Hillary shook his head. "I'm sitting in. If there's going to be a scrap—"

"Sorry, Hillary." Klaw grinned. "You have to stay out. You're still the sock salesman. If anything happens to Kerrigan and me, you'll be able to go on shadowing Lacosta till the Chief decides how to handle him."

He raised his voice, so that it rang over the lobby; at the same time he waved Hillary to one side. "You've got the wrong men, mister," he shouted. "We're not sock buyers. We're G-men. We're here to pick up a guy named Lacosta."

"Oh," said Hillary. "Sorry. I made a mistake." And he went back to his newspaper.

STEVE WINKED at Johnny. They advanced to the desk. The two men standing there watched Johnny and Steve through narrow-slitted eyes, keeping their hands in their pockets. But

Johnny Kerrigan, who had shoulders like a stevedore's and the strength to match, elbowed them out of the way.

"We're looking for Lacosta," he told the clerk, flipping open his F.B.I. identification card case. "What room?"

The clerk's eyes widened. "Room 1015—"

"Thanks." Johnny started to turn.

The other men in the lobby had begun to close in. The two whom Johnny had elbowed aside crowded in nearer Kerrigan, drawing guns from their pockets. But they underestimated Stephen Klaw.

It was not strange that they had done so, for the same error had been made often in the past. Stephen Klaw looked so slim and youthful that he could easily have been taken for a kid just out of college; it was natural that the two men at the desk should concentrate their attention on the one they deemed most dangerous, leaving the innocent-looking Steve to be taken care of by the others in the lobby.

They both pressed their guns against Kerrigan's side, and one of them murmured, "Sorry, dope, but nobody can see Lacosta for a while. Someone else has business with him first—"

That was as far as he got.

Steve Klaw hand-vaulted to the top of the counter, lashed out with his right foot. The toe of his shoe caught one of the two gunmen on the point of the chin, and the man went catapulting backward into those others who were moving toward the desk. They went down in a tangled heap.

The second gunman uttered an exclamation of alarm. He swung around toward Steve, bringing up his gun. Johnny Kerrigan drove a hard fist into the man's face, while Klaw, guns in hand now, turned to cover the clerk, in case that gentleman should have any notions.

The clerk was far from hostile. He seemed glad to see what was going on.

He said, "You're just what the doctor ordered. Those two muggs had me covered when you come in. They said they'd blow my top off it. I let out a peep. A bunch of them went upstairs to Lefty's room. What they're doing to the boss, I don't know."

Steve winked at him, and swung around, his two automatics ready. But Johnny Kerrigan already had the situation under control. He had a big service revolver in each huge paw, and he was leaning back, both elbows on the counter, covering the untangling mass of gunmen. There was a grin on his face as he waited for them to get to their feet.

"Of course," he said, almost coaxingly, "if any of you birds want to try for a gun, it would be fun."

But they weren't having any. They stood there, sullen, cowed, glaring murderously but helplessly at the two round black snouts of Johnny's guns.

"What say, Shrimp?" Johnny asked over his shoulder.

"Upstairs!" Steve said. "We may be late!"

He waved to Hillary, who had come out from behind his newspaper with a gun in his hand. "Think you can take care of this collection of rodents, Hillary?"

The New York G-man grinned. "I imagine so," he drawled. "I'll ring for a wagon and take them in for questioning."

Kerrigan and Klaw left Hillary in charge, and hurried to the elevator. There were two elevator shafts, but only one car was running at this hour of the morning. The operator stood in the open door, ashen-faced at what he had just witnessed.

"Up!" said Johnny.

The boy's hand was shaking; he could not close the door.

Johnny pushed him aside. He took the controls himself. Klaw stepped into the cage after him and waved to Hillary, who was already using the phone at the desk, keeping the disarmed gunmen covered.

Johnny closed the elevator door and sent the cage up.

"On your toes, Mope," said Steve. "There's a bunch of Black Troopers on the tenth floor. We'll have to come out shooting."

"Okay," said Johnny. "Here we are."

He stopped the cage, and drew both his guns again. "Here goes, Shrimp. See you in hell!"

"See you in hell, Mope," Stephen Klaw replied gaily. He slid open the door.

THERE WERE half a dozen men in the corridor of the tenth floor. The door of Room 1015 was almost directly opposite the elevator shaft where Johnny and Steve stood. Two of the Black Troopers were at one end of the corridor, and two at the other end, with drawn guns. Apparently their duty was to keep people away. As grim evidence of this, a man and a woman lay on the wine-colored carpet, down near the left end of the hall. Just to the right of the elevator was the body of Ray West, half-in and half-out of the broom closet.

The guards had done a thorough job, all right. And their

purpose was quite evident. It was to make sure that the third pair of Black Troopers would finish their work without interruption.

Those two men were kneeling in front of the door of Room 1015. One of them had a revolver in his hand, while the other was working with a set of tools which he had spread out on the floor at his side. He was using a drill which he had plugged in to one of the light sockets; it seemed that his object was to bore a set of holes around the lock.

The man didn't stop when Kerrigan and Klaw stepped out of the elevator. Apparently he was sure that his guards would protect him.

Those guards probably had not expected any important interference, for they were no doubt sure that the strong contingent downstairs would be enough to stop anyone in the lobby. But, when Johnny and Steve appeared, the gunmen swung into action. Their weapons began to blast fire and flame.

Kerrigan and Klaw stood side by side in the elevator doorway, Klaw facing to the right and Kerrigan to the left, their four guns playing a deep-throated symphony of death. They shot coolly, with deadly precision.

They had the advantage of surprise, as well as a certain psychological advantage which they always enjoyed. For to them, as well as to Murdoch, battle was always a joyful thing, and danger an element which they sought rather than avoided.

The ambassador had spoken truly when he had said that the Suicide Squad always seemed to be *seeking* Death. By all laws of average they should have been dead a long time ago. The term Suicide Squad was no mistaken appellation. Johnny Kerrigan had once punched a Senator's son in the nose; Dan Murdoch had shot a crooked croupier to death in a gambling house; and Stephen Klaw had told the chairman of a Senate Investigating Committee to go to hell when he had been asked why he had killed certain criminals rather than capture them alive. For such behavior, any other three men would have been summarily discharged. But such had been the records of Kerrigan, Murdoch and Klaw, that the Director had been able to avoid discharging them by pointing out that the public might resent it. So he had managed to keep them on the rolls of the F.B.I. on condition that they never be assigned to a routine case. They were kept on tap for cases which were too dangerous for a regular operative.

So they, and two other hellions, had become the Suicide Squad. Originally, there were five of them; then only four; then three—Kerrigan, Murdoch and Klaw. No one knew how soon there might be only two, or one—or none.

So, considering that they had no right to be alive anyway, Kerrigan and Klaw disdained to take shelter now, or to consider the odds. They stood there, shoulder to shoulder, trading shots with those five gunmen, giving a supreme demonstration of how Death avoids those who thumb their noses at it.

Their blasting guns seemed to be fired not by men of flesh and bone, but by two superbly coördinated fighting machines, grimly, inhumanly efficient. They did not shoot blindly and frantically, as did the surprised gunmen. They made each shot count, conserving their lead as a quota-motorist conserves his fuel. In answer to that blasting hail of poorly-directed bullets from the five gunmen, Johnny Kerrigan fired only twice with each revolver; and Stephen Klaw fired three times.

As if by magic, the blasting reverberations of the gunfire died away, leaving only rolling echoes down at the far ends of the corridor.

Five bodies sprawled on the wine-colored carpet. The man who had been working on the door with the drill did not realize just what had happened. So confident had he been that his fellows could control the situation, he hadn't turned from his task. Now, as the firing ceased, he kept drilling, and asked over his shoulder, "You got them, Karl?"

He used good English, except that his voice was a bit heavy, with a trace of a Teutonic accent.

"You got them, Karl?" he repeated.

Stephen Klaw grinned, winked at Johnny Kerrigan. He stepped swiftly to the side of the kneeling man.

"*Nein,* mine friend," he said. "They didn't got *uns!*"

The man gasped, and let go of the drill. It stuck in the door. He started to push up from his knees, but Johnny pressed the hot muzzle of his gun against the back of the fellow's neck.

"Stay right where you are, chum," he instructed.

The man froze, on his knees.

CHAPTER 4
THE FEMALE OF THE SPECIES

NONE OF the doors along the corridor was opened, which was testimony to the fear the blasting gunfire must have invoked in the breasts of the occupants.

Stephen Klaw disregarded the kneeling driller. He leaned close against the door of Room 1015.

"Open up, Lefty," he called. "Your troubles are over."

For a moment there was silence. Then a hoarse voice came from inside. "I know your tricks. You're the Little Gray Old Man. You wanna kill me. You wanna make me believe there was a gunfight out there. But I ain't falling for it. You ain't gonna get me so easy!"

Steve sighed. He tapped the kneeling man on the shoulder.

"Go on with your drilling, pal," he ordered.

The man cursed under his breath. Then he started to get up. "No! For you I do nothing!"

Steve shrugged. "It's okay by me." He turned to Kerrigan. "Put a slug through the back of his neck, Johnny. He's no good to us."

"Sure," said Johnny. "Glad to oblige."

He put the muzzle of his gun back against the fellow's neck.

"Don't shoot!" the man yelled. "I'll do it!"

Frantically he seized the drill and began to work.

"We better make this snappy," Johnny Kerrigan said. "We want to get hold of Lefty before the police come. What we have to do with him would hardly be approved by the police."

He tapped the kneeling man on the shoulder. "What's your name, friend?"

"Roeder," the other answered, without stopping his work. He had the circle of holes almost complete now, and was drilling on the last one.

"All right, *Herr* Roeder," said Johnny. "Suppose you tell us where to find the Little Gray Old Man."

Roeder turned to look up to Johnny, gave him a nasty grin. "Have no fear. The Little Gray Old Man will find you soon enough. You will not have to look for him."

He pulled the drill out of the last hole. The circle of holes was now complete around the lock. It was only necessary to punch out the whole section, and the door would come open.

Just then they heard the whine of cables in the elevator shafts. Steve glanced over toward the indicator. The cage in the second shaft was coming up. It was already at the third floor, moving rapidly. "Hold everything, Johnny," he shouted. "That may be the cops. Then again, maybe not!"

He sprinted to the elevator shaft, and smashed out the glass panel of the sliding door with the butt of his gun. He reached in and unlocked the door, slid it open. He leaned out into the shaft.

The roof of the cage was of glass, and he could see the occupants—the same gunmen whom Johnny and he had disarmed down in the lobby. Somehow, they must have overpowered Hillary and regained their weapons. They were coming up to reinforce their companions.

Steve smiled grimly. He pointed one of his automatics downward in the shaft, and pulled the trigger until the clip was empty, swinging the gun in a narrow arc in order to spray the bullets all around the interior of the cage.

The explosions rolled up and down in the shaft like the thunder of an imprisoned tornado. The sound of the shattering glass roof was drowned out completely, but Steve could see the havoc his fusillade had wrought. Only one of those gunmen in the cage had escaped being hit. And that one was not going to try to come any further. The cage shot downward again.

Steve nodded grimly. He turned back to Room 1015. Kerrigan had pushed Roeder to one side, and was waiting with his revolver pointed at the circular cut in the door.

Steve said, almost impatiently, "Shoot!"

Johnny pulled the trigger. The slug from the heavy calibre revolver smashed into the door, carrying the whole lock in with it. The door swung open itself.

Kerrigan took a swift stride forward—and stopped short on the threshold.

Lefty Lacosta was sitting in a chair at the far end of the room, facing the door. In his lap he cradled a sub-machine gun, one pudgy finger on the trip. His face was white and strained; there was sweat under his eyes. He had the look of a cornered animal.

"Don't come in!" he screamed. "I'll kill you!"

Johnny Kerrigan's revolver was pointing at Lacosta. He could have pulled the trigger before Lefty could have pressed that trip. But the object was to take Lefty alive.

"Listen, you dope," he said impatiently. "We're not working for the Little Gray Old Man. We've knocked off all his torpedoes. We're the F.B.I. You wrote us a letter, and we want to ask you some questions—"

"Yeah!" leered Lefty Lacosta. "And I'm your aunt's mother-in-law. You can't fool me. The Little Gray Old Man found out about that letter I wrote. He sent you guys to knock me off. But it ain't gonna be so easy. I'll take some of you with me!"

KERRIGAN WAS stymied. "You fool!" he shouted. "Come out here in the hall and take a look at all the nice dead Black Troopers. Would we kill our own men? I tell you, we're the F.B.I.!"

"Nuts!" said Lefty Lacosta. "You can't be the F.B.I. The F.B.I. ain't smart enough to buck the Little Gray Old Man. The F.B.I. won't even get near this dump till I'm dead. I'm sorry I ever wrote that letter."

His voice changed, became wheedling. "Look, fellow, can't you talk to the Little Gray Old Man. Tell him I'm sorry I wrote the letter. Tell him if he'll let me live, I'll never so much as peep about what I know."

But though his tone was wheedling, he never took his finger from the trip of the sub-machine gun. Apparently he had little faith in the quality of the mercy to be expected from the Little Gray Old Man.

Johnny Kerrigan kept on talking to Lacosta, stalling him along. He heard Stephen Klaw moving around in the corridor behind him, and he knew just what Steve was going to do.

It was one of the things that had made the Suicide Squad so deadly efficient—they had worked together for so long that they operated like a piece of well-oiled, high-geared machinery. Each could read the other's mind, could tell almost to a certainty what the other would do under a given set of conditions.

The result was that when they were in a tight spot, they didn't have to stop and consult each other, nor hold long conferences or councils of war. They acted, knowing that the others would support and complement the action.

Johnny Kerrigan couldn't see what Klaw was doing there behind him, but he *knew*. They had worked the trick before. It required split-second coördination, the most perfect kind of timing. So Johnny Kerrigan kept on talking, saying anything that came into his head, keeping an ear cocked for the signal from Steve.

"I tell you, Lacosta, you're wasting precious time. The police will be here any minute. Do you want them to pick you up? Wouldn't you rather come with me? I can prove I'm a G-man—"

He heard Stephen Klaw's low whisper behind him, to his left: "Okay, Johnny!"

Kerrigan stopped talking suddenly. He whirled on one toe, side-stepped back into the corridor, going to the right, out of the line of fire of Lacosta's machine-gun.

For a moment the doorway was empty. On the left side of the doorway, Stephen Klaw stood taut, holding up the corpse of one of the Black Troopers, which he had dragged over.

Lacosta shrieked, "What kinda trick you gonna pull? I warn you—the next guy that comes through that door—I'll spray him!"

"*Yow-ee!*" yelled Johnny Kerrigan. And at the same time, Stephen Klaw thrust the corpse of the Black Trooper in through the doorway, holding it up by the back of the collar for a second. Then he let go and ducked to one side.

He was none too soon, for Lacosta's machine-gun began to chatter. Slug after slug hit the corpse.

And then suddenly the machine-gun was still, leaving only the echoes of its spiteful clatter drumming through the air.

It was for that precise split-second that Kerrigan and Klaw were waiting.

Almost before the last burst had cleared the doorway, Klaw was on his way through, into the room, keeping low, bobbing and weaving like a broken field runner. He headed diagonally across the room to where Lacosta was sitting with the machine-gun.

Lacosta uttered a wild yell when he saw him; swung the machine-gun around to follow Klaw's erratic course through the room. Then, as if he were operated by an electric stop-watch which actuated him at exactly the proper instant, Johnny Kerrigan stepped into the doorway, both guns in his hands.

Lacosta was turned away from him, following Steve with the gun, frantically trying for a chance to get a bead and pull the trip.

Kerrigan fired once.

The slug spanged against the machine-gun, its force jerking the weapon around in Lacosta's grip. He almost jumped out of his chair. He let go of the weapon, and it clattered to the floor.

Johnny Kerrigan leaped across the room and grabbed him before he could move. Klaw stopped zigzagging.

He grinned at Kerrigan. "Nice shooting, Mope."

They got on either side of Lacosta, and each took him by an arm.

"The cops are on the way," Klaw told the shivering man, "and there's probably more of the Black Troopers after you. We're not going to waste time arguing. Our job is to get you out of here. You ought to be convinced we mean you no harm. My partner could have killed you just now if he'd wanted to. So—do you come along with us under your own power, or do we carry you out?"

"I'll come," Lacosta managed.

KERRIGAN AND Klaw virtually rushed him out of that room. They got into the elevator cage in which they had come up. They passed Roeder's inert figure in the hall, but left him there. Klaw had tapped him on the head just before they staged the rush on Lacosta's room, so that the man wouldn't be able to interfere.

Lacosta made no further protest as Johnny sent the cage downward. Below, they could hear police whistles, and the sounds of gunfire.

"That must be the cops arriving," Steve said. "They must have met up with some Black Troop reinforcements. The Little Gray Old Man wants you out of the way pretty badly, Lacosta."

Lefty Lacosta shuddered. "I should never of written that note. But I heard Cronin talkin' in the next office with the Little Gray Old Man, and planning something for the San Felix blackout. Maybe I am a crook, maybe I did do time. But I'm an American just the same, and I wasn't gonna let them get away with it. I wrote the note on a hunk of paper I got outta Cronin's wastebasket, and mailed it from Saint Louis, thinking you'd never trace it."

"Do you know any more about the Black Troop?" Steve demanded tensely.

"Not much," said Lacosta. "But I think I got a good idea where their headquarters might be."

"Wow!" Steve said. "We'll get you out of here alive—if we have to blow up the joint!"

Lacosta said accusingly, "This is *my* joint!"

"It won't be, if the Black Troop has its way in America!" Steve told him grimly.

Johnny Kerrigan, working the controls of the elevator cage, stopped it at the second floor.

Here, the corridor was crowded with guests of the hotel, who had been awakened by the gunfire. The shooting down below had increased in intensity, indicating that the battle between the police and the Black Troop was raging fiercely.

Kerrigan and Klaw led Lacosta down the length of the corridor, turned around the bend, and found the service stairs. They hustled him down to the main floor. They were now in the rear of the hotel, behind the kitchen. The shooting was coming from out in front. Back here everything was quiet. Even the kitchen help had disappeared.

Kerrigan opened the service door. Over his shoulder he said to Klaw, "Follow me, Shrimp. We'll have to scout around for a car, and make a quick getaway."

He had the door open now, and was peeking into the service

alley. He yelled, "Come on, Shrimp!" and dashed out into the alley. Steve followed, dragging Lacosta along.

There, parked in the alley, was a beautiful limousine bearing the emblem of the British Consulate.

Dan Murdoch was at the wheel of the car. Seated in the rear was Patricia Gilpin. She was handcuffed to the metal robe rack on the back of the front seat. Dan Murdoch was grinning like a kid. "All aboard!" he yelled. "Bus leaves in one second!"

Kerrigan and Klaw did not stop to ask questions. The back alley might be covered by the police or the Black Troopers at any moment. They piled in with Lacosta, swung the door shut; and Murdoch sent that car roaring out of the alley, his foot heavy on the gas.

The police and the Black Troopers were blazing away in the street, but they didn't have a chance to snap a single shot at that car, because it went streaking away like a black comet.

Murdoch swung west, then south, then west again, and slowed the car when they reached the waterfront. He brought it to a stop in a dark street, and turned to grin at Kerrigan and Klaw.

PATRICIA GILPIN was sitting, white-faced, her lips pursed, staring straight ahead. Dan nodded toward her. "Well, boys, aren't you going to ask me why I've been so rude to a lady?"

"All right," said Kerrigan. "We'll bite."

"Up at the British Consulate," Murdoch told them, "I kept an eye on Patricia, on account of what you had told me, Shrimp—about Bishopp's warning to look out for the dame with the ash-blonde hair. Well, she introduced me to the vice-consul, and left us. I made an excuse, and left the vice-consul and tailed her. She went downstairs to a public phone. I slipped into the next booth, and did a little listening. Guess who she was calling!"

"The Little Gray Old Man!" Steve hazarded.

"No. She was calling Mark Cronin. It seems that she phoned him from San Felix, just before we boarded the plane, and warned him we were coming for Lacosta. That's why the Black Troop was up there ahead of you. They were waiting for us, and then they were going to finish off Lacosta. This dame, my friends, is not what she seems to be. Her spy-ring got hold of the real Patricia Gilpin when one of the German raiders captured a British ship in the South Atlantic. The real Patricia Gilpin had lived in New Zealand all her life, and her uncle, the ambassador, had never seen her. So the spy-ring got this dame to imperson-ate the real Patricia Gilpin, and she came here and was accepted without question. That's how the Black Troop got its info!"

The woman posing as Patricia Gilpin sat silent, not denying anything.

"Over the phone," Murdoch went on, "she made a date with Cronin to meet him in a motor boat off the Battery. She was going to bring me along, on the pretext that she had a clue to the Little Gray Old Man, and get me on the boat. Then they were going to take me out to the headquarters of the Black Troop, and turn me over to the Little Gray Old Man.

"She spotted me when she came out of the booth," Murdoch said ruefully, "so I had to arrest her. I got the Consulate to lend me a car, and we came over to the Manx. I heard the shooting, and figured you'd be making a quick try for a getaway, so I pulled the car in the alley."

"Nice thinking, Dan," Kerrigan said.

"But that leaves us just where we were before," Dan said. "Because our lady friend won't talk. She won't say where the headquarters of the Black Troop is—"

"I can tell you that!" Lacosta cut in. "I heard the Little Gray Old Man giving Cronin directions. You go down the bay, along the Staten Island shore, till you see a house with three windows lit, on the shore. You blink your light seven times, then twice, and then you head in toward that house. The headquarters is somewhere behind that house on the shore."

"Let's go!" Stephen Klaw said gaily. "Drive on, Dan. You're going to keep that appointment with Cronin only it's going to be a sort of surprise party for him!"

"And let's hope," Johnny Kerrigan said, "that they've got Lord Chester there!"

CHAPTER 5
THE SPYMASTER OF THE AXIS

STATEN ISLAND lies athwart New York Bay, and comprises a formidable link in the chain of defenses of the great city, for Fort Wadsworth and Fort Tompkins—two modern and powerful fortifications—are located there on the island.

But it is also an ideal spot for the goings and comings of spies and unwanted saboteurs, for every vessel, going and coming, must pass its shores. On its east lies Brooklyn, across the Narrows; on its west lies New Jersey; and on the north lies Manhattan. South of Staten Island, ships come in for temporary anchorage in the lower bay, before moving up the Narrows to Quarantine. And there is ample chance for men to land from those ships on the fifteen mile coastline, or for men to leave those shores for ships at anchorage.

On the shoreline, almost directly opposite Fort Hamilton in Brooklyn, a pretty little stucco house nestles in the lee of a rising hill. At the top of the hill there is a stockade which is virtually invisible to anyone making his way on foot or by car along the shore road, for it is screened by a row of thick poplars.

The stockade itself is made of fine-meshed wire, ten feet high. Inside the stockade is what appears to be the country estate of a gentleman interested in racing, tennis and golf. In back of the huge, rambling house, there are outbuildings for servants, stable help and so forth. The tennis courts are situated at the right of the house, in the shade of other tall poplars.

Close inspection of this vast and peaceful looking estate would have revealed, however, that buildings which resembled stables were such only on the outside, the result of clever camouflage.

In reality they were one long, low hangar which housed two swift planes of the most modern design.

The golf course had a level stretch of two hundred yards, which made an excellent runway for landings and take-offs. This runway was of concrete, but it was painted green so that to an observation plane flying aloft, it looked like part of the golf course. The servants' buildings in the rear of the great house were really barracks, sufficient to house more than three hundred members of the Black Troop.

On the roof of the main house, two men with black arm-bands stood constantly on watch with high-powered glasses—one keeping his glass trained constantly on the sea, the other watching the tip of Manhattan Island at the Battery.

At eight o'clock in the morning, these two lookouts kept to their posts in spite of the beating rain which had begun to sweep down over the whole area.

It was the one who looked toward the south who first saw something of interest. He stepped into a small booth on the roof, which was equipped with a signal light and a speaking tube connected with the main floor of the house. He pressed a button, and a moment later a voice from downstairs said, "Yes?"

"I have just spotted the *Prinz Heinrich, Herr Colonel*," he reported, speaking in English. "She is standing out in the bay, flying the Brazilian flag, as arranged. The name painted on her bow is *São Tomás*."

"Good!" said the voice from downstairs. "Keep your glass fixed on her. Watch for flag-signals. We will not leave to board her until the quarantine officers have paid her a visit. After she reports that she has a case of smallpox aboard, the quarantine officers will forbid her to enter the harbor. She will be ordered to go on without stopping at New York, and then we will board her."

FIVE MINUTES later, the other watcher spotted something of interest going on at the Battery. He swore softly under his breath.

"Something is wrong with Cronin at the Battery, sir," he reported. *"Fräulein* Schiller, posing as Patricia Gilpin, was to meet Cronin at the boat, accompanied by Murdoch, whom she was to lure here."

"Yes, yes," the voice interrupted impatiently.

"Fräulein Schiller is there, sir, but with more than Murdoch. She has four men with her. One of the men is Lefty Lacosta. From the descriptions, I would say that the others are Murdoch and those other two devils of the Suicide Squad."

"So!" said the voice downstairs. "Something must have gone wrong at the Manx Hotel. Lacosta got away from our men. He knows this location. Let them come, Fritz. Watch them carefully, and report to me every five minutes. We will destroy the whole Suicide Squad this morning!"

Downstairs, in the book-lined study on the ground floor, the Little Gray Old Man flipped over the key on his desk closing the speaking-tube connection, and leaned back in his chair.

He looked across at Lord Chester Breedsley, who was handcuffed in a straight-backed chair, a husky Black Trooper on either side of him.

His eleven hours of captivity had wrought a terrible change in Lord Chester. But withal, he sat erect—though it took a visible effort to do so—and he still exhibited that innate dignity which nothing could destroy.

"Well, Lord Chester," the Little Gray Old Man said, "you have heard what is happening. If you entertain any hope that you may be rescued, please forget it. The Suicide Squad will be of no help to you. They are reckless men, and they will throw away their lives. You see how they come—three men alone, against these odds!"

"Perhaps they've arranged for help," Lord Chester said, speaking with difficulty. "Perhaps they've arranged for Navy planes to observe where they go."

"It would not help, my dear Lord Chester. Surely you don't think I would allow such a possibility to exist? If a plane is observed overhead, the three lights in the house on the shore will be immediately extinguished. And if any substantial force were to approach, the road up the hill is dynamited. We could set off the charge from this house, blocking the road completely. That would give me plenty of time to take off, together with my executive assistants, in the two planes. By the time the soldiers repaired the road and reached this place, they would find only my Black Troopers, whom I can easily spare. These three hundred are only a small percentage of the total number in the ranks of the Black Troop."

He paused, then went on. "No, my dear Lord Chester, there is no chance for you at all. Within an hour we shall take off in a power boat, and board the *Prinz Heinrich*. Under the Brazilian flag, we can cross the ocean in a convoy, escorted by British destroyers. In a week we'll be in Germany. But long before the week is over, you shall tell me everything you know!"

HE PRESSED another button on his desk, and a small door at his left opened, revealing a small room containing a complete radio sending and receiving outfit.

A man with earphones on his head came to the door. "Yes, *Herr Colonel?*"

"The *Prinz Heinrich* has arrived, Otto," the Little Gray Old Man said. "But do not use the wireless until I tell you. We do not wish to arouse suspicion at this time."

The man saluted, and returned to the radio room.

The rain was beating down heavily upon the roof, slapping vindictively at the windows. The Little Gray Old Man smiled in satisfaction. "Even if those three have arranged to be observed by a Navy plane, there will be little to see. An observer could discern nothing on the ground, from three hundred feet."

Lord Chester Breedsley stirred uneasily in his chair, a look of deep resignation on his face. Then he immediately squared his shoulders.

"Who are you, anyway?" he demanded. "I hear your men call you *Herr Colonel.* I gather that you are the head spymaster of the Axis. But you couldn't possibly be—"

The Little Gray Old Man nodded. "Indeed, yes, Lord Chester. You have met me before. But it is not your fault that you do not recognize me. Do you remember when you flew to Berchtesgaden with your former Prime Minister one day, two years ago? You were introduced to me then."

Lord Chester stiffened. For a moment all his bodily pain was forgotten as he stared at that wrinkled, smiling face across the desk.

"*Von Reichenstein!*" he gasped. "But—but it's impossible! Von Reichenstein was—"

"A younger man, eh?" the other supplied. "And nothing like the Little Gray Old Man, eh? Well—see for yourself!"

The Little Gray Old Man rose. As he did so, the stooped shoulders seemed to disappear; he appeared to grow in stature. He did something with the gray hair upon his head, and the wig came off, revealing a close-cut, Teutonic haircut. He stooped before the desk, and opened a small can of cream, which he applied to his face. Underneath that wrinkled old skin there appeared a younger, firmer face. A small eye-patch was placed over his left eye. He stood up smartly, and saluted, in the best Teutonic manner.

"At your service, Lord Chester!"

The British diplomat gasped. "Incredible!"

"Incredible? Not at all, my dear friend. In the secret service of the Greater Reich, nothing is incredible—and nothing is impossible. The poorest spy in our service is an adept at disguise, even in his natural self. You will note that there is nothing wrong with my eye, yet for years, as Wolfgang von Reichenstein, I wore this eye-patch, so that it became associated with me. Those who sought me always looked for a man with only one eye. Therefore, they never found me! As for the character of old Pappy Ricks, I had a double build up that character for me, years before your country thought that the Reich would ever be a menace to America. And now, Pappy Ricks is above suspicion. Even now, if something should happen to go wrong with our plans, the Little Gray Old Man will remain above suspicion and above reproach. Excuse me for a moment!"

He disappeared into another room, and was gone for less than five minutes. When he returned, he was clad in a Nazi uniform, with a swastika band on his sleeve. He bowed once more.

"As you see, I am now here in my own name, as Wolfgang von Reichenstein. If I should be captured, there will be nothing against me. The worst that your stupid officials could do to me would be to deport me to Germany. And I would return almost at once, with another name, and another face!"

THIS WAS all just a bit of braggadocio in which von Reichenstein was indulging. He was talking to a man who was his prisoner, and who would—as he thought—never be able to repeat a word of it. A spy is the loneliest person on earth, for he has no one in whom he can confide. Thus, when, he has an opportunity to boast before one who will never be in a position to violate the confidence, he is apt to make many revelations.

Von Reichenstein was no exception. But he was interrupted by the buzzing of the annunciator on his desk. He flipped over the key, "Yes?"

It was Fritz, the lookout, speaking from the roof. "The three devils have landed, *Herr Colonel*," he reported. "From what I can see, they have *Fräulein* Schiller and Mark Cronin handcuffed to each other. They have given Lacosta a gun. They are making their way up the road to the stockade."

"Good!" said von Reichenstein. "Signal for the gatekeeper to open the stockade door, and to hide. Let them come through, then close the stockade door."

He closed the annunciator, and pressed another button on the desk. Immediately the door opened, and a lieutenant appeared.

"Prechter!" he ordered. "Take a detail of troopers and deploy them on the grounds, with machine-guns. There are five men and a woman coming in. The woman is *Fräulein* Schiller. Kill the others, but try to avoid injuring her. She is valuable to us."

Lieutenant Prechter saluted and disappeared.

Von Reichenstein motioned to the two burly guards to move Lord Chester's chair nearer to the window.

"I shall let you have the pleasure of watching the destruction of your friends. I understand that this Suicide Squad is the most dangerous combination of Federal agents in America. I have already met Stephen Klaw. I should have liked to capture him alive and take him back to Germany. But I have no time for that, now. Watch!"

He pointed out of the window to the five figures who had come in through the open stockade door.

Lord Chester could recognize Kerrigan, Murdoch and Klaw, as well as the woman he had thought to be the Ambassador's niece. He groaned inwardly as he saw them advance toward the house, apparently unaware of the trap into which they were walking.

Just then, the roar of a plane's motor became audible from somewhere far overhead. At the same time, the annunciator buzzed again.

Von Reichenstein went back to the desk. It was Fritz, on the roof, reporting. "There are two planes overhead, *Herr Colonel*. From the sound, they seem to be Navy Bombers. But the visibility is zero. They can see nothing."

Von Reichenstein chuckled. "Very good. We will kill those three under the very noses of the planes that were supposed to cover them. And we shall then abandon this place, and take Lord Chester out of the country—also under their noses!"

He went back to the window. The small group had advanced about halfway to the house. In the dim light, through the beating rain, Lord Chester could see that four of the men were carrying small-arms, while Cronin and *Fräulein* Schiller were handcuffed to each other.

Von Reichenstein said tensely, "Another moment, now, and Lieutenant Prechter will attack. Watch!"

Lord Chester Breedsley heaved himself out of the chair with a violent effort. He hurled himself against the closed window. His shoulder struck the glass and smashed it outward. At the same time he raised his voice and shouted as loud as he could:

"Look out, Klaw! It's a trap—"

One of Lord Chester's burly guards struck him on the head with a gun butt. Lord Chester's shout died in his throat as he fell.

Dark figures appeared out of the shadows around the grounds, moving in toward Kerrigan, Murdoch and Klaw.

Von Reichenstein, at the window, cursed the guard. "Why did you hit him, you fool? You might have killed him. We want him alive!"

He stooped beside the unconscious Lord Chester to make sure he was not badly hurt, and thus he missed the next act of the drama in the courtyard.

He did not see the small Mills bombs which Kerrigan, Murdoch and Klaw took from their pockets. These were the new, modern type of Mills bomb, developed by the Army. They were one-fifth the size of the old Mills bombs, but the explosive they contained was two hundred percent more potent.

Each one of them had a pocketful, and they began to pull the pins and hurl them as fast as they could, as if they were throwing baseballs.

Small plumes of fire began to spurt up from the ground all about as those little bombs landed, and Black Troopers died where they stood. Wherever a bomb exploded, inflammable material continued to burn. Some of the bombs reached the outbuildings—those structures resembling stables but which were really hangars, and hot violet flame mushroomed out as gasoline tins exploded.

The grounds suddenly erupted into a bedlam of flame and gunfire as the remnants of the first contingent of Black Troopers, under Lieutenant Prechter, were joined by men hastily routed out of the barracks.

CHAPTER 6
DEATH FOR ALL!

PRECHTER HAD only taken a squad of two dozen men, thinking that would be ample to surprise and kill three fools. But now that he had discovered his mistake, he blew his whistle for reinforcements, and they came on the run.

In the center of the courtyard, Kerrigan, Murdoch and Klaw moved grimly toward the house, shoulder to shoulder, throwing grenades as they moved forward, and disdaining to crouch or to take cover from the desultory fire which the thoroughly surprised Black Troopers turned upon them.

It was ironic that the Black Troop, which had thought to lead the three into a death trap, were themselves trapped by this surprise move of the Suicide Squad.

It was unthinkable that three men had come prepared to fight three hundred. Even von Reichenstein, clever as he was, had thought that they were depending upon some outside force to follow them; that they were merely scouts, nosing out the hideout, and that they would take cover until the Navy plane could bring up assistance. And feeling that the Navy planes would be able to see nothing in this weather, he had counted upon eliminating the Suicide Squad swiftly. Even he had not guessed that Kerrigan, Murdoch and Klaw would seek battle with his whole garrison.

By the very nature of the reckless, suicidal action, they were successful.

Before allowing the bogus Patricia Gilpin to keep her rendez-vous with Cronin at the Battery, they had stopped at the New York F.B.I. office and provided themselves with grenades and Very pistols for flares. And Kerrigan was carrying a compact, portable radio transmitter on his back. They had contacted Naval Intelligence and arranged for the Navy bombers to fly over Staten Island. Knowing that visibility would be poor, they had arranged to send up Very flares, and Kerrigan had told them that they would send out a coded beam to guide the bombers down. The duty of those bombers, if the beam went out, was to dive and let go of their burden of bombs—to blast hell out of the place, to destroy it and everything in it.

That was as a last resort. They weren't going to use the portable radio to send that beam unless every other means failed. And the reason for it was the parting order from the ambassador: *If you can't save Lord Chester, he must die!*

That they, too, would die in the chaos caused by the big Navy bombs was a foregone conclusion. But they accepted that.

And now, as they advanced shoulder to shoulder upon the great house, they were calm, almost happy. For this was the way they had always dreamed of finishing it up—going out fighting, shoulder to shoulder, and taking as many of their enemies with them as they could.

Those grenades which they kept on throwing had spread a great circle of flame around them. Behind and to the right, the hangars were burning brilliantly, while ahead of them, some of the grenades which Johnny had heaved had caught on the main portico, tearing a great hole in the front of the building and starting a hot blaze.

Fifty yards from the house, they hurled the last of their grenades in through the windows. Then they made a dash for the building. Now they had their guns out once more, but they didn't shoot. They were saving their lead for what they would find inside.

They had left Lacosta with Cronin and *Fräulein* Schiller back at the stockade, not wishing to be burdened with them. And they were quite sure that they themselves would hold all the attention of the Black Troop for the next few minutes, so that Lacosta would not be molested.

They reached the house, sprinting through a hail of bullets.

One man with a machine-gun stood on the burning porch, waiting for them. But they were vague shadowy targets in the sweeping rain and the gloom, while the man was brilliantly silhouetted against the background of flame. Murdoch cut him down with a single shot, and as they swept up on the porch, Kerrigan stooped and picked up his machine-gun.

They swung into the burning house, still shoulder to shoulder, as part of the roof crashed in. It missed them by inches, but they didn't stop. They had glimpsed the two burly guards dragging Lord Chester out through a rear door.

They rushed through after them, but the guards with their prisoner had already disappeared across the grounds, into the barracks at the rear. And out of those barracks there came streaming the remainder of the three hundred Black Troopers. This last contingent had had more time than the others, and they were armed with machine-guns and grenades. They deployed and began to advance toward the house.

Kerrigan, Murdoch and Klaw stopped.

"Ugh!" said Johnny. "We can't make it. We'll have to signal the planes to bomb."

THERE, IN the lurid flames of the ruined house, they turned and looked at each other. Disregarding the warily advancing Black Troopers, they solemnly shook hands all around.

"Well, Mopes," Steve Klaw said, "this is it. When those Navy planes drop their loads, there won't be enough of us left to identify. Be seeing you—in hell."

"I'll be there, Shrimp," Kerrigan said with a grin.

"Me, too," said Murdoch. "It'll be hot down there—but no hotter than this!"

Then they swung inside, and Kerrigan started to set up his portable radio set, when Steve Klaw noticed the open door of the radio room. Part of one wall was gone, and the roof was burning beautifully, but the sending apparatus seemed to be intact. He tapped Kerrigan on the shoulder, and ran into the room.

Dan and Johnny followed him, and as he seated himself before the sending instrument, the first wave of Black Troopers came storming into the house.

"Go ahead, Shrimp!" Kerrigan shouted. "We can hold these babies till you get the beam out. Then you can lock the set and join us."

He and Murdoch opened up on the Black Troopers. Kerrigan pumped the machine-gun into the thick ranks of the enemy, while Murdoch fired his revolver coolly, like a sportsman picking off clay pigeons. And Stephen Klaw sat imperturbably at the sending set, clicking off the beam signal which would bring the bombers.

Never had three men set out to commit suicide in a more thorough or painstaking manner.

The first volley which Kerrigan and Murdoch fired into the enemy sent them sprawling back in swift retreat, leaving a dozen dead and wounded in the burning, ruined house.

"Well," said Murdoch, "that gives me time to reload. You got a full clip, Johnny?"

Kerrigan nodded. "I just gave them one burst. Looks like we can hold them till the Shrimp makes contact, all right!"

Klaw was ticking away at the key, sending out the coded signal repeatedly, and listening for the first response which would tell him that the bombers were on the beam.

But none of the three had noticed the figure with the black patch over one eye, who was ensconced behind the partially demolished closet wall.

Von Reichenstein had not accompanied Lord Chester across to the barracks. He had sent him under guard, but he had remained to destroy certain papers and codes in the secret closet behind the radio room. It was there that he had been crouched when the first of Johnny's grenades had struck. He had been about to emerge when the three had come back into the radio room. On hearing them, he had slipped back behind the closet wall.

He was directly behind Stephen Klaw. He stood there, with his gun raised, waiting for his chance. As long as Klaw was unable to contact the bombers von Reichenstein was content to wait, trusting to his own Black Troopers to storm this position and dispose of the Suicide Squad. He waited, with a smile of deadly hate on his face. These three had disrupted the orderly plans for his departure. He would now have to use an alternate plan, which meant crossing Staten Island with his prisoner, to another boat landing, where he had a reserve motor launch waiting. He only wanted to make sure that the Suicide Squad was destroyed before he left.

"I've got them!" Steve Klaw exclaimed, as he caught the coded buzz in his earphones.

Then came the voice of a Navy pilot, two thousand feet overhead: *"Calling Klaw! Calling Klaw! I have your signal. I'm on your beam. Keep sending. Here we come. I hate to do this, old man, but here we come. The Navy salutes you, Kerrigan, Murdoch and Klaw!"*

"All right, Mopes," said Steve. "The bombers are on the beam!"

He kept ticking the key in the coded signal, bringing the bomber down to destroy him, and he did it with a grim smile on his face.

At that moment, the Black Troop began their second assault. The troopers came charging in through the demolished front wall of the house, blasting away with carbines and machineguns. They must have refrained from using grenades because they knew von Reichenstein was in the house, and they did not wish to destroy him also.

Kerrigan and Murdoch opened up again, standing in such a way that their bodies protected Klaw from bullets. They wanted him to keep on sending until the last moment. Grimly they smiled to think that in a matter of seconds now, all this would go up in long spumes of smoke—as the heavy bombs landed.

But now von Reichenstein deemed it time to act. He must break that beam!

BEHIND STEPHEN KLAW, he swung his Luger down, and sent a shot into the batteries underneath the sending set. In the din of the gunfire, the shot went unnoticed. But Klaw at once knew that the set was dead, and he sensed, rather than heard, that the shot had come from behind him.

He kicked the table away, then sprang, backward, overturning the chair upon which he sat. He landed on his back. Above him, he saw von Reichenstein, smiling like a vicious gargoyle, and pointing his gun straight down at Steve's head.

Klaw had no gun in his hand. He knew that shot would get him. The Navy planes had already lost the beam, but if he lived he could use Johnny's portable set to contact them once more.

He must stay alive now—in order to die for a purpose!

Kerrigan and Murdoch had no time to turn around. The battle had become hot. The Black Troopers were pouring in fast, hoping by the sheer weight of numbers to get past the deadly barrage which Kerrigan and Murdoch were setting up.

Klaw did the only thing he could possibly do under the circumstances. He thrust both hands out backward, over his head, and caught one of von Reichenstein's ankles. Just as the spymaster fired, Steve yanked at his ankle.

Von Reichenstein slid forward on his heels, and the shot went wild. The spymaster landed on the floor on his back, alongside Steve. Klaw, who was slim and wiry, packed a punch flavored with dynamite. He twisted around on top of von Reichenstein, and let him have one square in face.

The back of the spymaster's head bounced against the floor. Steve hit him twice more, not hard enough to knock him completely out, but sufficient to make him too groggy to resist.

Kerrigan and Murdoch had become aware of what was happening behind them, and they backed up just a little. Out in front, the floor was littered with dead and dying, but the rush had been broken.

Half a dozen of the troopers had found shelter just outside the house, and were peppering away from there. This sort of thing couldn't go on indefinitely, for Johnny's clip was almost exhausted, and Murdoch was working on his last reserve round of bullets.

Steve Klaw grasped the situation in a glance, and sprang to his feet, dragging the semi-conscious von Reichenstein with him.

Johnny Kerrigan fired the last round from his machine-gun, and threw it away.

"I'll take him, Shrimp!" he shouted.

None of them knew that this was the Little Gray Old Man. But they had all seen pictures of von Reichenstein. They knew that, in his field, there was no one in higher authority. This was a windfall on which they well knew how to capitalize.

Relieved of the burden of the semiconscious spymaster, Steve Klaw took his two automatics out of his pockets. Murdoch picked up von Reichenstein's Luger. Then they flanked Johnny Kerrigan.

Kerrigan held von Reichenstein up in front of him with ease, like a puppet. And the three of them advanced that way.

A great shout of consternation went up from the Black Troopers as they saw their leader being used as a screen for the three devil-fighters. Shooting died down, then ceased. Those men with the black armbands retreated as Kerrigan, Murdoch and Klaw walked out of the burning building with their prisoner.

Outside, the whole area within the stockade was brightly illuminated by the flames. The fire had spread, so that all the buildings were sending up great geysers of fire into the heavens.

And by that light, the huge, graceful forms of five Navy bombers became visible. They were flying low, coming in from the east, and they had cut down low enough below the overhang to spot the fires.

One after another, those beautiful lords of the air came down along the runway. The squadron leader's plane, which had a red kerchief at the tail, sent a single burst of machine-gun fire high over the heads of the Black Troopers, and that was enough.

The troopers threw down their weapons and raised their hands.

STEVE KLAW found Lord Chester, half sitting, half lying on the ground, where he had been abandoned by his two burly guards.

Lord Chester got to his feet painfully, and looked at Stephen Klaw.

"God help me," he said, "I never thought you could do it!"

Steve helped him over to the plane, where Kerrigan and Murdoch had already brought von Reichenstein. The plane crews were already out on the grounds, rounding up the Black Troopers, in whom there was absolutely no more fight.

Commander Paine, the squadron leader, saluted Lord Chester. Then he solemnly shook hands with Kerrigan, Murdoch and Klaw, in turn.

"You three guys have a standing invitation to dinner at the Navy base," he said. "The boys will all want to see what you're made of. Personally, I think it's asbestos. Believe me, I was damned glad when we lost that beam. I wouldn't have been able to sleep for a month if I'd let our load down on you. Come over tonight. We'll celebrate with two cases of Scotch."

Klaw grinned and turned to Lord Chester. He motioned toward von Reichenstein, who was still groggy, but able to comprehend that all his plans had been knocked into a cocked hat.

"Lord Chester," said Steve, "in case you don't know it, this is the head spymaster—"

"I know it well enough!" said the British diplomat. "And I'll tell you something else. You don't have to look for the Little Gray Old Man any more. There he is!"

Swiftly, Lord Chester told them about the *Prinz Heinrich*, standing out in the bay, and one of the planes' radio operators communicated the information to the Naval base.

Lord Chester turned to Kerrigan, Murdoch and Klaw. "I want you three to fly back to Washington with me. There is nothing that the British Government won't do for you. And the ambassador will want to thank you personally." He glanced over toward where a couple of the Navy men were leading *Fräulein* Schiller and Mark Cronin away, with a smiling triumphant Lefty Lacosta behind them.

"The ambassador will want to thank you particularly for exposing his bogus niece. He'll want to see you at once."

Steve Klaw glanced at Kerrigan and Murdoch, who gave him the negative nod. Then they all three looked at Commander Paine, who seemed a bit crestfallen.

Steve grinned. He turned to Lord Chester. "Sorry, sir, but we have a date tonight—to drink the Navy under the table!"

—FOR TOMORROW WE DIE!

CHAPTER 1
KILLER'S LOOT

THEY WERE three tough-looking muggs. The big one had red hair and shoulders like a stevedore; the dark-haired one looked like an athlete, slender-hipped and long-legged, his carriage as lithe as a panther's; and the little one seemed hardly more than a kid, but hard as nails. The big fellow carried a small Boston bag as they got out of the taxicab in front of the Trafalgar Realty Company's store, just off Chicago's busy Loop District.

The little one kept both hands in his pockets, while he looked right and left up the street. He jerked his head at the other two, then all three men started toward the Real Estate office door.

"Hey, you guys!" called the cab driver. "You didn't pay me!"

The tall dark one grimaced, turning back. "Wait here," he said. "We ain't through with you."

"I'd rather get paid now."

The tall one came all the way back to the cab, stuck the palm of his right hand into the cab driver's face, and pushed him back in his seat.

"Listen, mugg," he said, "when I say wait—you wait!"

Then he turned around and joined his two companions. The three of them entered the real estate office.

A man inside the office had been watching them through the store window. He was a skinny fellow, with a sallow face and small eyes. He made a motion to someone in the rear, and four men appeared from the back of the store. They held their hands up close to their neckties, and the bulges under their armpits were quite evident. They were not at all at ease as they waited for the three tough-looking muggs to come inside.

The big one entered first, followed closely by the other two. He stopped, and stared contemptuously at the group awaiting them.

"Reception committee?" he growled.

"Yeah," said the little one. "A reception committee of nice pink-and-white lillies. They mope around this phony real estate office and wait for three guys from New York to lift the biggest load of ice in town!"

The skinny man with the small eyes glanced nervously at his reinforcements, and then spoke to the three strangers.

"Now listen, you guys," he said, "I told you when you called up that I didn't know what you were talking about."

The big mugg with the red hair grunted. "Baloney. We was tipped off that this is the joint where we contact Louis LeGrand. So trot him out. We got to see him, and time goes fast. We're so hot the street sizzles wherever we walk. Now don't waste our time."

"But I tell you, we don't know any Louis LeGrand. Who is he?"

"Hah!" said the big mugg. "Don't be funny. Everybody knows that Louis LeGrand is the fence that buys what no other fence can touch. And we got what he buys, right here in this bag. Now, do you do business with us—or do we tear this joint apart to find him?"

The skinny guy snarled, "You ain't got a chance. Scram before we go to town on you—"

He didn't quite manage to finish the sentence, because the little mugg—the one who looked like a tough kid—stepped in, flicked a left to the skinny guy's cheek, then followed it with a flooring right to the button.

"Don't ever talk like that to my pal," he said. "He might get sore and really hurt you."

THE SKINNY guy was out cold, and that seemed the signal for which the other men in the real estate group had been waiting. They went for their guns.

But abruptly, all four of them froze. Both the big red-headed mugg and the tall, dark-haired one were holding revolvers in their hands.

The dark-haired mugg said sweetly, "Don't let's get foolish, boys." The four gunmen looked sheepishly from one to the other, and decided not to be foolish....

The youngish mugg shoved his hands back into his coat pockets. He said callously. "These guys don't know the right time. Let's knock 'em off and blow for New York. We can sell the ice there. We don't need this Louis LeGrand—"

Just then, a stout man waddled from the rear of the store. His dark blue suit must have cost a hundred dollars, and his tie couldn't have sold for less than ten. He had a diamond in the tie as big as a flashlight bulb. He was clean-shaven, and his hair was freshly barbered.

"Gentlemen, gentlemen," he said reprovingly. "Why make trouble? I'm sure there's nothing we can't straighten out without resorting to guns."

The dark-haired mugg kept his revolver trained on the group of real estate men, but he shrugged.

"It's up to you, pal," he said. "We come in here trying to do some honest business, and your gun-bums try to give us the rush. Nobody can do that to us!"

"I think I can straighten this whole thing out," said the fat man. "In my private office."

131

"That's better!" the big redhead grunted.

The little fellow who looked like a kid grinned. He seated himself on a desk near the window, keeping both hands in his pockets, and facing the four cowed gunmen.

"Go ahead," he told his two companions. "I'll just stay here and keep these dopes company."

He winked at the four he called dopes. "In case you guys are wondering what I got in these pockets, you can find out very easy—just by making a quick motion that I don't like. But if you stay very still, and don't make any trouble while my two pals are inside, you won't have to worry."

His two companions followed the fat man into the private office at the rear. Once inside the private office, with the door closed, the fat man sat behind his desk. He frowned up at the two muggs.

"Now look, you guys," he said. "I'm Dunn. You've probably heard of me."

"Sure," said the redhead. "We've heard of you. Fatty Dunn, the best finger man in the racket. You fingered jobs for Dillinger, and for the Osprey boys, and for a bunch of others. You always managed to stay in the clear. Nobody ever got a thing on you. And now you're respectable—you're in the real estate business. That's what the cops and the public think. But we know different. We know you're fronting for Louis LeGrand."

He plopped the Boston bag down on the desk. It was so heavy it almost cracked the glass top.

"We got ice to sell. Plenty of it. We've come to LeGrand because we want a good price."

The fat Mr. Dunn looked pained. "Of course, I must tell you boys that I don't know what you're talking about. I'm in the real estate business, and I never heard of this Louis LeGrand. But if you boys have anything to sell—and it's honest stuff—I'd be willing to look at it. You'd have to give me a bill of sale, of course."

"Sure, sure," said the redhead. "Here. Take a look at this, first."

From his pocket he took a newspaper. He spread it on the desk, with page one on top. The headline read:

$1,000,000 JEWEL ROBBERY!

At six o'clock this evening, just before closing time, three bandits invaded the premises of the exclusive Parisienne Jewelers and forced Joseph Frere, the manager, to open the main vault, in which was stored the million dollar collection of rare jewels which the company had purchased only today. The police and the F.B.I. are investigating. Mr. Frere has been taken to an undisclosed hospital to be treated for shock, and no one has been permitted to see him...."

The fat Mr. Dunn did not bother to read all the way through.

"I heard it on the radio," he said. His eyes were bright and sharp as he looked at the two muggs, and then down at the Boston bag.

The redhead grinned. He opened the bag, turned it upside down, and dumped the contents on the desk.

Dunn drew in his breath sharply. Jewels—large and small, with breathtaking lustre and sheen—cascaded from the open mouth of the bag. There were emeralds and sapphires, diamonds and amethysts, some in settings, some loose.

"There it is, Dunn!" said the redhead. "One million dollars worth of it. How much will LeGrand pay for the lot?"

The fat man licked his lips, a strange look of respect in his eyes.

"You boys pulled that job!" he said. "You knocked off the Parisienne Jewelers. They're right around the corner. And you have the guts to wander around in the Loop, while every copper in the city is looking for you!"

"So what?" said the dark-haired mugg.

CHAPTER 2
THE KING OF CRIME

THE BIG redhead stirred impatiently. "All right, let's quit the gabbing and get down to business. We want to sell this junk and lay our hands on the dough."

Dunn sat back in his chair, pretense swept aside now.

"You guys don't expect to get cash on the line for a job like this?" he asked slowly.

"Why not?" demanded the redhead. "LeGrand has the dough."

"Sure, but you ought to know how he works. He has a job cased, and then he authorizes it. After it's authorized, he keeps the cash ready to pay off when the stuff is delivered to him. But in this case, he didn't even have time to order the job. The Parisienne just got this stuff in today. You must realize that LeGrand does a nationwide business. He authorizes maybe fifty jobs a week, all over the country, and the cash to pay off for them has

134

to be transferred from the main office. Besides, he always sets a cash value on the stuff when it's cased, and the price is arranged in advance. I don't know how much he'd be willing to pay. This stuff would have to be sent to his appraiser, for a valuation. It would take time."

"Where's the appraiser?" the dark-haired mugg demanded. "We'll take the stuff to him ourselves."

Mr. Dunn smiled. "The appraiser we're now using happens to be in New York."

"Give us the address, and we'll take it there."

"You're crazy," Dunn said. "Every guy with a shield between here and New York will be looking for you guys. You don't seriously think you could get this stuff to New York without being picked up!"

The dark-haired one smiled wolfishly. "Provided there's not more than a dozen guys at a time trying to pick us up, we'll get through all right!"

Dunn looked at him appraisingly. "Tough, aren't you?"

"Tough enough for this racket," the dark-haired one told him.

Dunn seemed puzzled. "Guys like you, I should have heard of before. You must be in the racket a long time. Just who are you?"

The big redhead grinned. "I'm A. Shlitz. He's B. Shlitz. The little guy outside entertaining your pals is C. Shlitz."

Dunn made a wry face. "You don't trust me, eh?"

"We trust you," said the redhead, "like we trust a rattlesnake."

"Will you let me take this stuff to LeGrand so he can look it over?"

"If we go along."

"Impossible! Nobody sees Louis LeGrand. Even I have never seen him. He talks to me in a dark room, and keeps me blinded with a spotlight in my eyes all the while I'm with him."

The big redhead sighed. He reached for the jewels. "It looks like we can't do business—"

"Wait," Dunn said. "There should be a way we can work this out. I know for a fact that Louis LeGrand is interested in this stuff—he can sell it for a good price in South America. He told me to have some of the boys line up the job, but you guys beat us to it."

"Well, snap it up," said B. Shlitz.

"I'll see if I can contact him," Dunn murmured. He picked up the phone, and dialed a number so that they couldn't see what it was. He held the receiver away from his ear, while it rang at the other end. He counted five rings, and then hung up.

"What the—" said B. Shlitz. "If he ain't even in—"

"Don't worry," Dunn told him. "He's in. That phone rings in a certain drug store. The clerk in the drug store doesn't answer it, but he counts the rings. Five is my signal. Each sub-organization has a different signal. New York has three, San Francisco has seven, and so on. The clerk goes to the street door and makes a signal. He doesn't know who he's making that signal to. It might be somebody in the street, it might be someone in the houses across the way, or it might be a guy with a telescope on some roof a mile away. He holds up the same number of fingers as there were rings on the phone, so Louis LeGrand knows which city or which sub-headquarters called. Fifteen minutes later, he calls back that number. That's how we contact him. Nobody ever sees him."

"Boy!" exclaimed B. Shlitz. "That's some system. He must be a genius!"

"I guess he is," said Dunn. "I'm telling you boys about this signal stuff, so you'll realize how powerful LeGrand is. He's got agents in every city in the country. Sometimes the guy or the dame walking right next to you in the street is working for Louis LeGrand. Take a tip from me: never cross him; and always do what he says. You never know where you'll get it, or who will do it—"

He was interrupted by the phone's ringing. He picked it up quickly, and said, "Dunn speaking."

AT THE sound of the voice at the other end, he began to talk, respectfully. "Parisienne, boss," he said. "I got it here. It's offered. I don't know the guys, but they're okay."

He paused and listened for a moment, while the voice at the other end spoke. Then he covered the mouthpiece and said to the two muggs, "The boss offers a hundred and fifty grand."

"Sold!" said the redhead.

Dunn nodded in satisfaction, and spoke once more into the phone. "It's okay, boss. They'll take it. Yeah, I got the stuff right here on my desk."

He hung up, and looked at his two visitors. "The dough will be here in ten minutes. In the meantime, I got to count this stuff. There was supposed to be sixty-four items."

He set about counting the precious stones.

The dark-haired mugg went to the office door and opened

it. He looked out, and saw that his pal out there had everything under control. He was sitting comfortably on the desk, talking pleasantly to the four men, who were standing stiffly, their hands at their sides. The skinny guy was sitting up groggily in a corner, but making no trouble.

The dark-haired mugg grinned. "Okay, Shrimp," he called to his pal. "You can let the dopes relax now. Everything is sweet. We're closing the deal."

"Just to be on the safe side," the tough-looking kid replied, "I'll stay out here for a while."

"When a guy comes with the dough," the dark-haired one said, "let him through. He's bringing a hundred and fifty grand." He went back into Dunn's private office, where Dunn had finished counting exactly sixty-four items.

The redhead looked admiringly at Dunn. "Say, that's some system this LeGrand has. How does he manage to get such heavy dough up on the line in ten minutes? Where's it coming from?"

Dunn smiled secretively. "LeGrand has this racket down to a science. He finances a bunch of gamblers on the side, under another name. Don't ask me what it is, because I don't know. But whenever he wants to transfer cash, or get it up quick, he phones one of the gamblers in the town where he needs the dough, and the gambler delivers it."

"Listen," said the redhead, "I'd like to do some more business with this LeGrand. We got a couple jobs spotted for New York. How will we contact him there?"

"You better get LeGrand's okay on the jobs before you pull

them. He may just have authorized some other mob to do that particular piece of business, and then you'll run into trouble. When you want to get an okay in New York, call Harbor 5-4900, and say you want to talk to Mr. Jones. The girl who answers will say, 'What is it about?' and you'll say, 'It's about a cow.' She'll say, 'What about this cow?' and you'll say, 'It's ready to jump over the fence.' *Fence*—Get it? Then the girl at the switchboard will tell you to call a certain number where Mr. Jones can be reached that day. He keeps shifting every week, so you have to call the Harbor number each time you want to reach him."

"I see," said the redhead. "Harbor 5-4900. I'll remember that!"

They heard heavy footsteps outside. A knock sounded at the door.

"Come in," Dunn called.

The door opened, and a dapper man walked in, with a brief-case under his arm.

"Hello, Rispard," Dunn said. "I see you got the money."

Rispard nodded. "I came right over as soon as I got the phone call from you-know-who. Here it is. A hundred and fifty grand."

He opened the brief-case on the desk. His eyes flickered momentarily as he noted the heap of jewels, but he said nothing. He took out sheafs of bills, and laid them carefully on the desk.

"It's all in small bills," he said.

Dunn counted it, with the redhead and the dark-haired one watching him.

"It's all here," he said.

"That's fine!" the dark-haired one said. He took out a revolver

139

and covered Dunn. At the same time, the redhead took out a revolver and poked it into Rispard's ribs.

"Gentlemen," he said, "you're under arrest!"

"What?" said Dunn. "I don't get it."

"Arrest," said the redhead. "Sorry to disillusion you, but my friends and I are not the Shlitz Brothers. We're Special Agents of the Federal Bureau of Investigation. The names are Kerrigan, Murdoch and Klaw. We're arresting you on the charge of being active accomplices of one, Louis LeGrand, and for conspiracy to receive stolen goods across state borders."

"**NOW WAIT!**" Dunn said. "This stuff is the swag of the Parisienne robbery—"

"You can bet your sweet life it is," said Kerrigan, the redhead. "But we're not the men who staged the robbery. We caught the three men who pulled the job, less than an hour ago. We shot it out with them, and they won't do any more shooting, ever. We've always wanted to get a line of LeGrand, and this was too good to pass up."

Murdoch—the dark one—went over and opened the door.

"Okay, Shrimp!" he called to Steve Klaw, the one who looked like a kid. "We broke the news gently."

"Me, too!" Klaw grinned. He had lined up the four weaponless prisoners with their faces to the wall and their hands in the air.

"I'll call the office," Murdoch said.

Still dazed, Dunn watched him dial the number of the Chicago F.B.I. Field Office.

"My Gawd, what a sap I am!" he whispered. "Kerrigan and

Murdoch and Klaw. The Suicide Squad! And I tried to do business with them!"

Their pictures never appeared in the papers if they could help it, which might have excused Dunn for not having recognized them. The name he had mentioned for them—The Suicide Squad—was one they had earned over and over again.

This was the kind of assignment they usually got—the job of going up against big odds, with little chance of success. They were a special roving squad, who never got a routine assignment; they were kept in reserve, to be used when the Chief of the F.B.I. would ordinarily hesitate to ask for volunteers. The three hellions welcomed the odds, and they welcomed the danger. It had often been said that they seemed to be seeking death, and that for that very reason death avoided them. Nevertheless, there had once been five in the Suicide Squad. Then four. Now three. Today or tomorrow, there might be only two, or one—or none. But whenever and however the end came, one thing was sure: Kerrigan, Murdoch and Klaw would go out fighting, on their feet; and they would take a goodly number of their enemies along with them.

This bold impersonation of theirs today had been Steve Klaw's idea. The Chief had reluctantly agreed over the long-distance telephone, after the capture of the three bandits who had held up the Parisienne Jewelers. Luckily, they had been able to keep that news out of the papers, but there had been a great element of risk; for although they were pretty sure that the bandits had been working without authorization from LeGrand, there was always the possibility that LeGrand's men might know who had pulled the job, and would not fall for the hoax.

But Dunn had walked right into the trap.

They hadn't hoped to catch LeGrand himself—it was known that LeGrand never conducted any of his negotiations in person. But the idea was to cripple his organization as much as possible, to sting him so badly that he would be brought out into the open and tempted to make some ill-considered move that would enable the Suicide Squad to get a direct crack at him. Thus far, the plan had been tremendously successful.

It was proved further by the phone call; that came in to the real estate office while they were busy loading the files and the papers into an F.B.I. truck.

Stephen Klaw answered the phone when it rang.

"Hello," came the voice at the other end. "I want to talk to Kerrigan, or Murdoch, or Klaw."

"This is Klaw," Steve said.

"This is Louis LeGrand. I'm calling to congratulate you. That was a clever bit of business you put over. And quite costly to me. It destroys my whole Chicago organization, and I pay out a hundred and fifty thousand dollars in addition. I compliment you on your daring."

"Thank you," said Stephen Klaw. "It's nice of you—"

"Don't bother to trace this call," LeGrand interrupted. "I assure you it'll get you nowhere."

"I'm not tracing it," Steve told him honestly. "What I want to know, is how you found out about this little business so fast."

LeGrand chuckled. "I have many ways. I also have many

agents, and many sources of information. I merely called to tell you that you and your two friends are so clever—" LeGrand's voice lost its suave smoothness and became bitter with hatred— *"so clever that you've got to be eliminated!"*

"That's a good joke, LeGrand," Steve said.

"I've never failed to keep a promise or a threat," LeGrand told him. "And I swear that if you come to New York, you and your friends will be dead ten hours after you arrive. I'm going to stage your deaths in an extremely spectacular manner, so that everyone will know that LeGrand is not the kind of person who can be trifled with."

Thanks," Steve said politely. "Kerrigan, Murdoch and I will be in New York tomorrow morning."

"Then you die tomorrow!" LeGrand told him, and hung up.

Steve put the receiver down, and looked up at Kerrigan and Murdoch, who had been listening to the conversation as best they could.

"We stirred the old boy up, all right, mopes," he said, grinning. "We've been invited to attend our own murders in New York."

"I'll phone for plane reservations!" Dan Murdoch said.

CHAPTER 3
MURDER PREVIEW

T HE NEWS item was boxed on page one, indicating that the City Desk had considered the story quite important.

G-MEN MURDERED!

John Kerrigan, Daniel Murdoch and Stephen Klaw, three Special Agents of the Federal Bureau of Investigation, were found hanged by the neck last night in the Sporting Goods Department of the Crescent Department Store. Their hands and feet were tied, and they had been strung up side by side, in one of the elevator shafts on the Fifth Avenue side of the store. The cage had been run up to the top floor, and the ropes by which they were hung were fastened to the underside of the cage.

Kerrigan, Murdoch and Klaw had been dead about five hours when they were discovered by the night watchman, who found the door of the elevator shaft open at the ninth floor and investigated.

The police have no clue to the identity of the wholesale murderer, except for a card found upon the body of each G-man. These cards bore no printed or written matter, but each had a picture of a cow jumping over a fence.

Thus, at last, is ended the brilliant career of three of the most colorful members of the Federal Bureau of Investigation, known as the Suicide Squad, because of their repeated defiance of death. This time, though, their luck did not hold....

The Chief of the Federal Bureau of Investigation had flown up to the New York office overnight and the newspaper was spread out on his desk. He was drumming with his fingertips on the desk-top, while gazing reflectively at the three men.

"None of you three hellions looks very dead to me," he said.

Stephen Klaw grinned. "If you'd seen the meal Johnny Kerrigan just put away, Chief, you'd be sure he isn't dead!"

Kerrigan, husky and powerful, with shoulders like a steve-dore's and a pair of hands that could rip a telephone book apart, merely scowled more darkly.

"Listen, Shrimp," he said to Klaw. "For a guy your size, you didn't do so bad, either. Nobody has to show you how to eat—"

"Now, now, boys," Dan Murdoch interrupted. He was the best-looking of the three—dark and lithe, with the slender hips and the long legs of an athlete. "Let's not squabble about a little food. After all—" he gestured toward the newspaper on the desk—"we're supposed to be dead!"

The Chief immediately grew sober. He tapped the news item with his forefinger. "You've certainly succeeded in bring-ing Louis LeGrand out into the open. The three men who were found hanging in the Crescent Department Store had forged credentials on them that must have cost LeGrand a pretty penny. They were three bums, picked up in the street. And they were murdered in cold blood, just to get this item in the paper!"

"LeGrand has a ghastly sense of humor," Dan Murdoch said, "but I've got to hand it to him. He works fast when he gets mad. Still, what's he got to gain from a gag like this?"

His answer came quickly enough. There was a knock at the door, and a clerk brought in an envelope addressed to the Suicide Squad.

Kerrigan took the post-marked envelope, slit it open, and drew out a single sheet of expensive bond paper. On it was a message typed in capital letters.

"Not a bad bit of business!" he said, and handed the letter to the Chief. It read as follows:

KERRIGAN, MURDOCH AND KLAW
c/o F.B.I., NEW YORK

HOPE YOU ENJOYED READING YOUR OBIT-
UARIES, EVEN IF THEY WERE AHEAD OF TIME.
THE THREE CORPSES IN THE CRESCENT ARE A
PREVIEW OF THE MANNER OF YOUR DEATH. I
INTEND TO KEEP MY PROMISE TO THE LETTER.
EAT, DRINK AND BE MERRY—FOR YOU'LL BE
DEAD BY THREE O'CLOCK.

BEST WISHES FOR A PLEASANT TRIP TO HELL.

THERE WAS no signature, but underneath the message there was a carefully drawn pen-and-ink picture of a cow jumping over a fence. The cow had its head turned, peering back as it jumped, and its face was that of a gaunt, emaciated devil, with a pair of vicious, malevolent eyes.

"Some valentine," Stephen Klaw muttered.

The Chief's eyes were bleak. "We must stop LeGrand—and stop him soon. Or else he'll have the whole country laughing at the F.B.I. He's conducting his fence operations on a nationwide scale, right under our noses. You boys did a nice piece of work in Chicago, but that isn't enough. We've got to destroy LeGrand and his entire organization!"

"Before he destroys us!" Dan Murdoch murmured.

The Chief shuffled through papers on his desk. "Professor Thaddeus Gedney died two weeks ago, in the Schuyler Hospital," he said, referring to the papers. "Death was the result of a heart attack. He had been examined by two well-known heart specialists, Doctors Glenville and Esmond. He was duly cremated. But after the cremation, we received a tip from a stoolie that Gedney's death was tied up somehow with Louis LeGrand. The stoolie was sure that LeGrand was responsible for Gedney's death, but he didn't know any more than that. The only connection we can see, is that Professor Gedney—who held the Chair of Antiquarian Research at Columbia—was a noted authority on jewels and precious stones. He had been retained as consultant by almost every auctioneer of precious stones in the city as well as by most of the wealthy collectors who purchased jewels. Now, if we could only tie his death to LeGrand!"

"Well," said Stephen Klaw, "we might as well work on that, as on anything else—till three o'clock."

"There's a possibility," said the Chief, "that Professor Gedney was murdered because he knew too much. Suppose you take the Schuyler Hospital, Steve; you, Dan, go see Doctor Esmond; and Johnny, you take Doctor Glenville. Check on all angles. In the meantime, we'll watch for something to break."

"Let's try the number that Dunn gave Johnny—Harbor 5-4900," Steve suggested. "Dunn is still in jail in Chicago, and there's a chance that he hasn't been able to tell LeGrand that he gave the number to us. Maybe we can establish the contact—"

"But if Dunn *has* managed to warn LeGrand," the Chief pointed out, "you'll be walking into a trap!"

Steve grinned. He picked up the phone, and dialed Harbor 5-4900.

The phone rang for a moment, then a girl's voice said, "This is Harbor 5-4900. Good morning."

"Good morning, sister," said Klaw. "I want to talk to Mr. Jones—about a cow."

"What about the cow?" the girl's voice asked.

"It's ready to jump over the fence."

There was a second's silence. Then the girl said, "Phone Gorham 2-2200, and ask to speak with Mr. Lamson, the patient in Room 714," and hung up.

Steve had jotted down the number and the name. The Chief, looking at it, exclaimed, "That's the number of the Schuyler Hospital!"

Steve's brows raised a notch. "So we contact Mr. Lamson— let's not forget that name!"

He dialed Gorham 2-2200, and when he got the connection he said, "May I speak with Mr. Lamson, in Room 714?"

He waited a moment, listening, then he said, "Thank you," and hung up.

"Well," he said, "I guess we don't see Mr. Lamson."

"You mean he's lammed?" Kerrigan asked.

Steve shook his head. "Mr. Lamson is dead. He died five minutes ago—a heart attack!"

"I think," Dan Murdoch said dreamily, "that we are beginning to crowd Louis LeGrand's toes."

"Either that," the Chief said, "or he's setting a trap for you three at the Schuyler Hospital. Perhaps we should raid the place—"

"Not that, sir!" Murdoch exclaimed. "You can be sure that LeGrand is clever enough to have provided for a raid—if this is a trap. I think the best way to handle it is for only one of us to go. That might put him off guard. Now I'll be very glad to volunteer—"

"Nix!" said Klaw. "The Chief already assigned the Schuyler Hospital to me!"

Murdoch sighed, and took out a coin. So did the other two members of the Suicide Squad. The three of them tossed, caught the coins on the back of their hands. Kerrigan uncovered first, heads. Murdoch uncovered next, and he, too, had heads. Steve Klaw smiled broadly as he revealed his coin. It was a tail.

"Too bad, Mopes," he said, grinning.

"The Shrimp always wins the toss," Kerrigan complained. "I bet that coin of his has two tails!"

Klaw hastily put the coin back in his pocket. "Well, Mopes, I'll be on my way. After you make your calls on Glenville and Esmond, don't forget to make a stop at the Crescent Department Store. Take a look at those three bodies. We should at least get a glimpse of the preview of our murder."

"Give my regards to Lamson's corpse," Kerrigan called after him.

THE TAXICAB let Stephen Klaw off in front of the Schuyler Hospital, and he stood at the curb a moment, looking the place over. It was a small hospital, not a public institution, but one of the hundreds which are privately operated in the City of New York. However, it must have enjoyed a staff of prosperous physicians, to judge from the many sleek, chauffeur-driven limousines bearing M.D. plates which were parked at the curb.

Steve had both hands dug deeply in his coat pockets as he studied the clean white building, which was sandwiched in between taller apartment houses. The hospital itself was only seven stories high, whereas the houses on either side were tall, modern apartment houses.

There was a strange aura of quiet and mystery about the place which piqued Steve's interest. At first he couldn't determine what it was that gave him that feeling. Then he realized what it was—the windows were not transparent glass; they were made of some opaque substance.

He kept his hands in his pockets, and went inside.

The lobby was spic and span white tile and polished bronze. A girl in a trim white uniform smiled at him from the information desk. An interne was chatting with two nurses near the cashier's window, and a distinguished-looking physician with a small, neatly trimmed Vandyke beard was talking softly into a house phone near the switchboard. Everything looked respectable and professional. In fact, it looked *too* much so.

Steve said to the girl at the information desk, "You have a Mr. Lamson here, in Room 714?"

The girl nodded, suddenly sympathetic. "Are you—a relative, perhaps?"

"No," Steve said. "Why?"

"Mr. Lamson has just—died. The poor man had a heart attack. I always feel bad when the relatives come, and I have to tell them a patient has died. You understand. It's so—so sad."

"Sure," Steve said. "I understand. Can I see the body?"

"Well," she answered doubtfully, "only relatives and close friends are permitted—"

150

"I was his father's closest friend," Steve said, straight-faced. "In fact, he sent me a telegram just a few minutes ago."

"I suppose it's all right. Just a minute, please." She tapped a bell on the counter, and the pleasant-looking young interne who had been chatting with the nurses came over.

"Dr. Rodney," the girl said, "this gentleman was a friend of poor Mr. Lamson, the patient in 714. He'd like to see the body."

The young man gave Steve a friendly, sympathetic glance. "Of course. I think it's still in 714. What is your name, please?"

"Klaw," said Steve. "Stephen Klaw."

He watched the young interne's face, but could detect no change of expression.

Steve was out in the open now. He had decided that this was no longer a time for masquerading. From now on it would have to be an open fight to the finish. If they were waiting for him here, baiting a trap, he didn't want any pussy-footing around.

But the name of Klaw seemed to have no special significance for the interne.

"Come this way, Mr. Klaw," he said, and led the way across the lobby, toward the elevator at the rear. On the way they passed the doctor with the Vandyke beard, who had just finished his telephone conversation.

"By the way, Mr. Klaw," said the interne, "this is the physician who was treating Mr. Lamson. Perhaps you'd like to talk with him?"

"Thank you," said Steve.

The interne completed the introductions. "Doctor Dean, this

is Mr. Klaw, a friend of Lamson's. I thought you might tell him something of the case."

"Certainly," said Doctor Dean. He watched Steve with bright, keen eyes, through shell-rimmed glasses. "It was a most puzzling case, Mr. Klaw. The poor man had a heart which, by all the rules of medicine, should have stopped beating years ago. It was amazing to me that he survived so long. Did you know about his heart?"

"Can't say that I did," Steve told him.

"As long as I am still here, I'll be glad to go upstairs with you, and explain just what we did."

THE THREE of them got into the elevator and rode up to the seventh floor. Doctor Rodney, the interne, led the way to 714, while Doctor Dean kept alongside of Steve, explaining in long and technical terms the other ailments which had afflicted Mr. Lamson.

Steve listened gravely, his hands still in his pockets. He noted that every step they took was oddly silent; not even a whisper echoed from the walls. The hospital was completely sound-proofed, in the most modern manner.

At Room 714, Rodney pushed the door open and led the way in. Steve followed, the bearded Doctor Dean behind him.

A body lay on the bed, covered entirely by a white sheet. But Steve had no time for more than a quick glance at it. Rodney closed the door and stood with his back to it, while Doctor Dean opened his black physician's bag and took out a revolver. His eyes were glittering like the points of two daggers as he trained the revolver on Steve.

"Now, Mr. Klaw," he said softly, "I shall be pleased to explain just how people die in this hospital—"

Steve didn't wait for the doctor to finish, or to fire the revolver. Instead, he shot him with the automatic which he was gripping in his own right-hand pocket. He didn't bother to take the automatic out; he simply fired through the cloth, aiming up.

The explosion was loud and sharp in the room. The doctor was lifted just a trifle off his feet, then he toppled backward without pulling the trigger of his gun.

Steve didn't wait to see the doctor's body hit the floor. He took the other automatic out of his left-hand pocket, swung around to face the interne, and covered him.

The interne was pulling a small pistol out from under his white uniform coat, but when he saw the automatic in Steve's hand he stopped, grinning sickly.

"Disgusting, isn't it—this murder business," he said pleasantly. "Sometimes it works in reverse."

"Quite so," Steve said politely. "And if you'll permit me to say so, your boss, Louis LeGrand, ought to be ashamed of himself for sending a couple of amateurs like you and this Doctor Dean to handle me. I consider it an insult."

"Oh, you're mistaken," said Rodney. "We're not amateurs by any means. We're about the best in the business. But even the best of us are bound to make a mistake once in a while. We underestimated you. You looked so young and inexperienced that we became a little careless. It was unfortunate that you happened to be holding those two guns in your pockets; otherwise, I assure you, you would be dead right now."

153

"Too bad you can't do it over again."

"Oh, but we shall!" the bogus interne told him. "Unfortunately, my friend, Dean, won't have the opportunity. But I, and others, will try again. Next time, we won't be so careless."

Steve grinned. "Do you think you're going to get another chance? You're going to be in a cell for a long time—"

Rodney laughed. "LeGrand will see to it that I don't stay in jail very long. I may not even reach the prison. He has so many connections."

"You wouldn't care to talk, would you?" Steve asked.

"Definitely, no," Rodney answered firmly.

Steve sighed. "Well, I've enjoyed our little chat immensely. And now, if you'll pardon me—"

He dropped the automatic back in his pocket, stepped in swiftly, and smashed a right to the interne's jaw. It connected with the force of a riveting machine, and Rodney's head snapped back. He teetered on his feet for an instant, then collapsed.

Steve grunted, and rubbed the knuckles of his right hand. He went through the man's pockets quickly, but found absolutely nothing. He grunted, took out a pair of handcuffs, and snapped them on the unconscious interne's wrists.

Just then, he heard the sound of swift movement behind him. He whirled, still crouching, and saw that the corpse on the bed had thrown off its sheet and was sitting up, gripping a heavy revolver.

Steve didn't wait to ask for explanations, or to wonder at miracles. He threw himself forward in a dive which carried him under the bed, just as the pale-faced corpse fired the heavy revolver. The gun thundered in the room, drowning out the other's exclamation of annoyance and anger at Klaw's unortho- dox action. It threw both legs over the side of the bed, evidently intending to get another shot at Steve.

Klaw seized both of the supposed corpse's ankles, and yanked hard. He seized the man's gun wrist in both hands, and twisted it hard. The corpse yelled in pain, and let go of the revolver, claw- ing at Steve's face with its other hand. Steve kept his grip on the wrist, and twisted all the way around. He felt a bone snap. The corpse whimpered, and abruptly stopped fighting.

Steve grunted, and climbed out from underneath the bed, brushed himself off. He kicked the revolver over into a corner of the room, and looked down to meet the eyes of the corpse, who had been fully dressed under the hospital bedsheet. He was a thin, wiry man, tough-looking and hard. But his face was screwed up in pain as he held onto his broken arm with his good hand.

"I'm sorry I had to do that," Klaw said. "But you wouldn't stop fighting."

"It's quite all right," said the corpse. "I would have done as much to you under the circumstances."

"You're Lamson, aren't you?"

"That's the name I'm using this week. I wish you'd get me a doctor for this arm."

"Sure," said Steve. "This hospital must be full of doctors. I'll find you a good one."

He took one link of the handcuff off Rodney's wrist, and dragged the unconscious interne over to the radiator. Then he helped Lamson over to the radiator, too. He ran the link of the handcuffs behind the radiator pipe, and clicked the free cuff around Lamson's good wrist, securing both of them.

"Don't fret," he said, going to the door. "I'll be back soon."

"I wouldn't mind if you came back on a stretcher," said Lamson.

Steve grinned. "I'll do my best not to oblige you!"

He walked down toward the elevator, in the deserted hall. Apparently the scene had been set for Steve's easy and quick elimination, and he wondered if the whole hospital, including the staff of doctors, was in cahoots with Louis LeGrand. In a moment he had his answer.

CHAPTER 4
THE LADY LEAVES SUDDENLY

H E WAS passing Room 702, which was next to the elevator shaft. The door of 702 was closed, and not a sound came from within. He was almost past it, when something banged violently against the door.

Steve stopped short, both hands in his pockets. He came back, and stood close to the door, listening. There was another bang against it from within.

Hospital doors never have locks. This one—although in a very queer kind of hospital—was no exception. Steve took his left hand out of his pocket, pushed the door open, and stepped into the room.

The four people who were struggling in there stopped. Two

of them were nurses, in white starched uniforms; the third was a heavy-set man who wore the white jacket of an attendant.

The three of them had been concentrating their attention upon the fourth occupant of the room, and Steve recognized her immediately as the pleasant girl who had greeted him at the information desk.

It was obvious what they had been trying to do. They had a straightjacket half on and half off her, and they had been trying to hold her still so they could lace her into it. There was tape over her lips.

She must have been putting up a terrific fight for the faces of both nurses were scratched and bleeding, and the male attendant had blood on his forearm where she had apparently bitten him.

At the moment when Steve stepped in, the weak side was getting the worst of the argument. The girl had been thrashing around on the floor, and had managed to hit the door with her feet a couple of times. But now they had her down good and proper. One of the nurses was sitting on her stomach, the other was sitting on her legs, while the male attendant was wrapping the straightjacket around her.

They all stared at him as if he were a ghost.

Steve said mildly, "I hope I'm not intruding."

"Not at all." The white-jacketted attendant recovered quickly. "Come in and give us a hand with this little spitfire. We have orders to leave the hospital in ten minutes, and we caught her trying to tip off the F.B.I. over the phone. This little she-devil still has plenty of fight left in her. I would have knocked her out, but we don't want her unconscious. We have to question her when we get her to the other place."

"What other place?" Steve asked.

"Number Three," the attendant told him. "That's where we're transferring. This place is finished." He suddenly looked up suspiciously at Steve. "Say—I haven't seen you around—"

"It's all right," said Steve. "I was sent down from Chicago. Come on, I'll give you a hand with the girl."

The girl had stopped struggling momentarily, and a flicker of hope had entered her eyes when she had seen Steve. But now, hearing what he said, the hope died away, and was replaced by a glint of fighting fury. She threshed her legs about in a desperate effort to dislodge the two nurses, but it was to no avail.

The attendant cursed violently, and returned to the task of subduing the struggling girl.

"Okay," he called to Steve. "Come and wrap this jacket around her!"

"Glad to oblige," Steve said. He stepped around the nurses, took an automatic out of his pocket, reversed it, and tapped the attendant none too gently behind the ear with the gun butt.

The man grunted and fell forward, on top of the struggling girl.

The two nurses leaped erect in sudden alarm.

Steve smiled at them, reversed the automatic once more, and pointed it in their general direction.

"Don't compel me to get rough with you ladies," he said.

They stood quite still, holding their hands stiffly at their sides.

Steve nodded, and bent down and helped the struggling girl out of the jacket.

She heaved a sigh of relief, patted her uniform into place, and smiled at Stephen Klaw.

"Now I'm a lady again. Thank you for what you did. They laid the trap for you, knowing you'd come here either alone, or with one of your friends. You're Klaw, aren't you?"

"That's right," he said.

"I'm Gloria Mason," she told him.

"You don't look like a crook," he said. "How come you're working for Louis LeGrand?"

She dropped her eyes before his intent gaze. "I—I can't tell you about that. But I'm not working for LeGrand any more. I—I couldn't stand the idea of your being killed by those cold-blooded murderers. So I tried to phone the F.B.I., and they caught me at it. Will you get me out of here?"

"Sure," said Steve. He looked at the two nurses. "If you two ladies will accommodate us by stepping into this straightjacket, it will save a lot of trouble."

THEY GOT both nurses into the canvas jacket, putting one arm of each into a sleeve. It was just wide enough to go around the two of them. Gloria Mason helped to lace the jacket tight, then they left the two nurses sitting on a chair, and made for the door. The nurses weren't very comfortable, wrapped together like that, but Steve had seen enough in here to make him lose all sympathy for them.

Out in the corridor, all was silent. No sound came from the room where he had left the unconscious Rodney and the wounded Lamson with the dead Doctor Dean.

Gloria Mason looked around in bewilderment. "I—I don't understand it. There were patients in every room on this floor, only an hour ago. And now it's so quiet."

Steve went down the hall, from door to door, pushing each one open and peering in. There was not a soul in any of them, except in 740, the last room on the other side of the hall, directly opposite the elevator. In that room there were three dead bodies, laid out in a neat row on the floor, each one with a bullet hole in the forehead.

Gloria Mason, peering in alongside Klaw, uttered a gasp of shocked dismay.

"Those are three of the doctors on the staff!" she exclaimed. "Doctor Glenville, Doctor Stephens, and Doctor Esmond. They—they've been murdered! But—but why—"

Stephen Klaw laughed bitterly. "Because their usefulness

to Louis LeGrand is over. Don't you see? LeGrand is through with this hospital. He knew that once he used it as a trap for me or my friends, the F.B.I. would be swarming all over it. So he arranged to evacuate all of his own men from here, to some other hospital perhaps. These three doctors may have been unwilling or unwitting tools of his. Maybe they knew too much. Anyway, he had them executed."

He took her by the arm. "Come on. Let's see how fast we can get downstairs. That attendant said they were going to take you along. Maybe there's a truck or an ambulance down there, waiting for you."

He pushed the elevator button, and kept his finger on it. He saw the indicator start to move as the cage ascended. It reached their floor, and the door started to slide open.

The operator began to speak before it was all the way open. "Better snap it up. There's only three minutes to go. Where's Rodney and—"

He almost choked on his words as he got a glimpse of Steve.

Klaw grinned, stepped into the cage, and hit him hard, square on the button.

The man staggered backward, leaned against the wall for a moment, and then came back, flinging rights and lefts.

Klaw sighed, got out his automatic, and clipped him along the temple with the barrel.

"Sorry," he said. "I haven't the time to fool around with you."

He stepped over the man's prone body, waited till Gloria Mason got in, then sent the cage down.

The lobby was just as deserted as the rest of the hospital.

161

"Wait here," Steve said to Gloria. He hurried over to the switchboard, plugged in a line, and dialed the number of the F.B.I. Field Office. The moment he got his connection, he spoke swiftly, without wasting words. "Klaw talking. Send a raiding squad pronto to the Schuyler Hospital. Pick up prisoners in 702 and 714. They're all in the pay of Louis Le Grand. Hold them incommunicado, and keeps the news out of the papers so bail can't be arranged. Move fast. I'll contact you later!"

He hung up, took Gloria's arm, and led her to the front door. There was nothing out there—no truck, no ambulance, no one.

He frowned, and turned and raced with her across the lobby toward a small side door. This opened out into an alley. Sure enough, there was an ambulance pulled up out there, with the back doors open and waiting.

Peering out, Steve saw the figure of the driver in the front seat. The man was glancing impatiently at his wrist watch.

Steve pushed Gloria out into the alley, and followed her swiftly.

"Get in!" he ordered, indicating the ambulance. She obeyed swiftly, climbing up inside, and Steve followed.

"Moe, is that you?" the driver yelled from out front. "What kept you? You got the dame?"

"Yeah!" Steve grunted.

"Ready to shove off?"

"Yeah!" Steve closed the ambulance doors with a bang, and latched them on the inside.

"Okay," called the driver. "Here we go!"

THE AMBULANCE started, pulled out of the alley, and swung west.

The blinds were pulled all the way down on the side windows, so that it was dark and gloomy here in the interior of the ambulance. But Steve Klaw could make out the dark bulk of a figure lying on the floor near the front. He made his way over there, with one hand on the wall to balance himself against the crazy swaying of the ambulance as the driver raced wildly through the streets.

Steve knelt beside the figure on the floor. It was a small, thin man, whose hands and feet were tied; he was gagged and his eyes shone in the semi-gloom as he stared up at Steve.

"What—what is it?" Gloria Mason asked, coming up behind him.

Klaw moved aside so that she could see.

She took one look, and put a hand to her mouth to suppress a gasp. "It—it's Professor Gedney! But he died last week. They cremated him!"

"He must be a salamander then!" Steve said. He gripped Gloria's arm tightly. "Are you sure this is Professor Gedney?" he whispered, careful that the driver out front couldn't hear.

"Yes, yes. I saw him when he was admitted to the hospital. And I remember him. He was a friend of—of father's. He visited our house years ago when I was only a kid, and dad introduced me to him."

"Is your father a professor too?" Steve asked.

"No." She didn't tell him any more.

Steve took out his pocket knife, cut the bonds that held

Professor Gedney's wrists and ankles, then helped get the gag out of his mouth. The man was so weak, he could barely talk.

Steve put a hand on his shoulder. "Take it easy, Professor. I'm glad to see you alive. And surprised. They filed a death certificate for you."

"They—they buried someone else in my place!" Gedney managed to whisper. "They were holding me prisoner for good." He shuddered.

Steve frowned inquisitively.

"Until they should have no more use for me. I—I'm an authority on precious jewels. They—they made me appraise their swag—"

"Then you've met LeGrand," Klaw said sharply.

"Yes. But—but I didn't see his face. We talked—in a dark room—with a spotlight shining in my eyes—"

"Listen here," Gloria Mason interrupted, tapping Steve on the shoulder. "What I want to know is, where are we going now? What's the idea of riding in this ambulance?"

Steve grinned. "We're letting the driver take us to the new hideout—headquarters Number Three, according to what the attendant said."

They could see the back of the driver's head, through the glass partition. He turned and peered inside once or twice during the wild ride, but he couldn't see much more than the outlines of their figures, because of the darkened interior. Now he began to slow up, and in a moment the ambulance came to a stop.

Klaw lifted the blind on the side window. He peered out, then whistled softly. They were in a side street, just off Park Avenue, opposite an alley which served as the service entrance of the ultra-swanky shop on the corner. The name of the shop appeared on the plate-glass windows:

HOUSE OF PIERRE, LTD.
Purveyors of Rare Jewels

THE DRIVER turned around now, and pushed back the sliding glass partition. He peered inside, but Steve could tell that he still couldn't see very much.

"This is it, Moe," he said. "You go in the alley and ring the bell. Then we'll wait out here till they tell us it's okay to pull in the alley. Be sure that dame and the professor are gagged good. We don't want them screaming out in the street."

"Is this headquarters Number Three?" Steve demanded.

"Sure. You know—"

"The House of Pierre, Ltd.?"

"Sure. Say, what's come over you? You don't sound—"

"You guessed it, pal," Steve told him. "I don't sound like Moe because I'm not Moe."

He stuck his face out through the opening, so the driver could get a good look at it. Also, he stuck out the barrel of his automatic.

"Just keep driving, my friend," he said softly. "Or if you'd rather, I'd be glad to shoot your head off, and take the wheel myself."

"Who—who are you?"

"All you have to do is drive, pal," Klaw said. "Skip the questions. Turn left at the corner, and head downtown."

"Where are we going—"

"To F.B.I. headquarters!"

The feel of the cold muzzle at the back of his neck worked wonders with the driver. He tooled the ambulance down the street, and turned the corner, heading south on Fifth Avenue.

Gloria Mason plucked at Steve's sleeve. "Aren't you going to investigate that House of Pierre, Ltd.? It must be another of LeGrand's headquarters. Maybe you'll find—"

She stopped suddenly, clamping her mouth shut, as if she had already said too much.

"Find what?" Klaw asked sharply.

"I—I don't know. I—I just thought you might find a lead that would help you catch LeGrand...."

She said it weakly, and her voice trailed off, leaving the sentence unfinished, as if she knew that Klaw knew that she had really intended to say something entirely different.

"Look, lady," Steve said over his shoulder. "You're not telling me everything you know."

The girl made no reply.

Professor Gedney moaned, and she knelt by his side in the dark, obviously welcoming the opportunity to escape Klaw's questions.

Steve shrugged. There would be plenty of time to get her to talk, at F.B.I. headquarters. With the automatic touching the driver's neck, he directed him through the city traffic to the F.B.I. building.

The huge garage devoted to the storage of cars exclusively for the use of Federal Bureau of Investigation agents was active with arriving cars, bringing with them the prisoners taken in the raid on the Schuyler Hospital. The driver of the ambulance pulled inside.

Steve spoke to Gloria Mason over his shoulder. "Get the doors open."

He heard her moving toward the rear of the ambulance, and unlatching the doors, then he heard them swing open.

"All right," he said to the driver. "Stay right where you are till I get out."

He backed around Professor Gedney, and dropped to the floor behind the ambulance. The driver was sitting tight behind the wheel, not making any effort to escape. But it was not in him that Steve was interested at the moment. It was the girl. He looked around the garage—and Gloria Mason was nowhere in sight!

CHAPTER 5
BANNERS FOR THE BRAVE

"AND SO, sir—" Stephen Klaw was finishing his report to the Chief—"I thought it best to leave the House of Pierre unmolested, so that LeGrand will continue to think we know nothing about it. In that way, we may still trap him."

"You did well, Steve," the Chief agreed. "We'll keep that ambulance driver incommunicado, give him no chance to get word to LeGrand. And I'll place the House of Pierre under surveillance,"

He turned to Professor Gedney, who was seated in a chair

next to Klaw's. The three of them were in conference here, while the prisoners taken in the Schuyler Hospital raid were being fingerprinted and questioned in other offices.

"Now, Professor, if you feel strong enough to talk—"

The professor nodded eagerly. "First of all, I want to thank Mr. Klaw for effecting my release. It would have lasted a long time indeed, if he hadn't found me in that ambulance. You see, I was feeling indisposed two weeks ago, and I went to consult Doctor Dean, who is—was, I should say—supposed to be an authority on stomach ailments. He suggested that I enter a hospital for observation, and named the Schuyler Hospital. I agreed."

Gedney paused; a shudder ran through his emaciated frame. "From the moment I stepped into that horrible place, I was lost. LeGrand needed an expert to appraise the tremendous amounts of loot that were offered to him for sale. You may not know it, but he has received the swag of almost every major robbery which occurred in the United States within the past year. I know, because the stuff was brought to me to appraise, and I recognized many of the precious stones. I had seen most of them before, in museums, and in private collections I'd been asked to appraise. Two days after I entered the hospital, they announced that I had had a heart attack, and was extremely ill. Since I have no close relatives in New York, there was no one to raise embarrassing questions. Those friends who called were told that I must not be disturbed, and to make the story sound more plausible, two heart specialists were compelled to issue statements that they had examined me. I believe their names were Glenville and Esmond. It seems that Louis LeGrand had some sort of hold upon these physicians, by which he could compel them to issue those statements."

Stephen Klaw nodded. "LeGrand used them as long as he needed them. Then he liquidated them. There was another one, too—Doctor Stephens. But go on, Professor. Let's hear the rest of it."

"They brought me jewels every day, for appraisal," Gedney went on. "And they kept announcing that I was growing worse from day to day, until last week, when I 'died.' They cremated, in my place, the body of someone whom they had liquidated. It was their intention to keep me a prisoner forever; to make me their corporation appraiser, so to speak. Louis LeGrand visited me once, and talked to me in a darkened room, with a spotlight in my eyes. He told me that if I appraised the stuff honestly he'd release me after a year, with a small fortune as payment for myself. I knew he was lying. He would have killed me when he was through with me, as he did the others. But I pretended to believe him. I asked him why it was necessary to have all that material appraised, and he said that he was disposing of it in South American markets, and that he had to know its exact value, in order not to be cheated. He also said that in the future, all swag would be brought to me for valuation. In addition, since I was familiar with most of the precious stones in the possession of museums and private owners, he would be able to consult me in advance as to their value, so he could set a figure on them *before* they were stolen."

"Had LeGrand consulted you about the Parisienne collections?" Steve asked.

"Yes. Yesterday morning he called up to ask me what the jewels were worth. I told him that the estimate in the newspapers was quite correct, that the sixty-four pieces were easily worth a million dollars."

"I see," said the Chief. He turned to Klaw. "What about that girl, Steve—Gloria Mason?"

"I haven't had much time to check on her, sir," Steve said. "But I've discovered that her father was the well-known auctioneer, Obadiah Mason, who disappeared three years ago, with four hundred thousand dollars worth of uncut diamonds which he was supposed to auction off for a Dutch syndicate the next day. There's been no trace of him since."

The Chief looked inquiringly at Professor Gedney. "Did you know Obadiah Mason?"

"I did, indeed. He consulted me on many occasions, as did most of the diamond auctioneers. My opinion was that he was an honest man. I was quite surprised when he disappeared. I didn't know he had a daughter, though."

"Could it be possible, Professor," Steve asked, "that Obadiah Mason is really Louis LeGrand?"

GEDNEY SMILED tiredly. "Offhand, I should say that Obadiah Mason did not have the qualifications of criminal genius which LeGrand seems to possess. I—"

He was interrupted by the telephone. The Chief picked it up, listened for a moment, then handed it to Klaw.

"For you," he said.

Steve immediately recognized the voice of Gloria Mason.

"Mr. Klaw!" she said in a low, tense voice. "Please forgive me

170

for running out on you. There was something I—I had to do—something I couldn't tell you about."

"Can you tell me about it now?"

"I must, because I need help. I can't do it alone. But you must promise me something.

"What is it?"

"If I help you to get Louis LeGrand—you must promise me that if my father—is found to be involved with him—you'll give him immunity."

"I can't promise anything like that," Klaw told her. "That would have to be for a judge and jury to decide. All I can offer you is my promise to help him to the best of my ability."

"Would you arrest my father even after I helped you?"

"I can't promise anything," Steve said. "Your father might even turn out to be Louis LeGrand."

"No! That's impossible."

"Nothing is impossible."

"Then you won't promise—?"

"I'm sorry."

"Goodbye."

"Goodbye," said Steve.

"Wait!" she exclaimed.

Steve held onto the phone, sitting tensely, with the Chief and Professor Gedney watching him.

"All right," she said weakly, at last. "I'll help you—on your own terms. Can you meet me in twenty minutes?"

"Where are you?"

"In the Greer restaurant, on Park Avenue, across the street

from the House of Pierre. I'm watching three men here in the restaurant who seem to be waiting for someone from the House of Pierre. I've seen one of them before, at the hospital. I'm sure he's connected with Louis LeGrand."

"All right," Steve said. "I'll be there in twenty minutes."

"Hurry," she urged. "One of them is waiting just outside the booth here. I don't know if he just wants to use the phone, or if he's suspicious of me."

"Stay in that restaurant till I get there," Steve told her. "It's a busy place. They won't try anything in there."

The Chief and Professor Gedney had been able to hear the girl's voice over the phone, so Steve didn't have to relay the conversation to them when he hung up.

"I'll put a cordon around the House of Pierre," the Chief said.

"Please don't, sir!" Steve begged. "Louis LeGrand has so many channels of information, and such an efficient observation system, he'll know about the cordon. If he's in there, he'll find some means of getting out. Let me tackle this alone. I only wish I had Kerrigan and Murdoch along. I wonder where they are—"

The phone rang again, and Steve automatically picked it up.

"Hiya, Shrimp!" It was Dan Murdoch.

"Hiya, Mope!" said Klaw. "Listen, I was just hoping you'd turn up. I got a swell lead, and I wanted to let you in on it. I was feeling sorry for you—moping around at the Crescent Department Store, and checking on those doctors, while I had all the hot stuff. So if you want to meet me—"

"That's what I'm calling you about, Shrimp. Johnny and I ran into some pretty hot stuff ourselves, over at the Crescent, and we have a swell lead, too. Johnny thought we ought to give you a break and let you in on it. And believe me, Steve, our lead is plenty hot. Take a tip from me, and come right over and meet us."

"Where are you?"

"We're at the Greer Restaurant, right across the street from a joint called the House of Pierre, Ltd. It's a jewelry house—a swanky place—"

"*The House of Pierre!*" Steve almost choked on the words. "Have you got that lead too? That's my lead! And the Greer Restaurant! That's where I was going!"

"Now isn't that funny!" said Dan. "How the hell did you get hep to the House of Pierre? We got it by snooping around the Crescent Department Store—tagged the manager of their jewelry department as an ex-con named Poldi. Pelham, he calls himself now. Johnny and I cornered him in the men's room, and we put the fear of the Lord into him. He broke down and confessed he's been working with Louis LeGrand. He's been slipping some of the hot stones into his department, and selling it over the counter. Johnny and I put the pressure on, and he mentioned the House of Pierre. So here we are, in the restaurant across the street."

"I'll be right over," Steve said. "I'm supposed to meet somebody there."

"Make it snappy," Murdoch said, "because we're watching a dame in here who looks suspicious, and we want to tail her if she leaves. She's wearing a nurse's uniform, and she seems to be awfully interested in the House of Pierre. She just made a phone call from this booth—"

STEPHEN KLAW started to laugh out loud, winking at the Chief and Professor Gedney. "Listen, you mope," he said to Murdoch, "that dame is the person I'm going to meet at Greer's! She just told me that she's watching three suspicious-looking guys in the restaurant. That's you and Johnny and your friend Poldi!"

"Well, I'll be damned!" Murdoch growled.

"Hang on," Steve told him. "I'm on my way!"

He hung up, grinning.

"Now wait," said the Chief. He glanced at his watch. "Do you realize that it's just nine hours since you arrived in New York?"

"I hadn't stopped to figure it out, sir—"

"Well, *I* have. In one hour, the deadline set by LeGrand for your death will be due. I'm sure LeGrand intends to move heaven and earth to keep his promise. He must, to maintain his prestige in the underworld. Now it's entirely possible that this lead to the House of Pierre is another trap, just as the Schuyler Hospital was, It looks too pat to me—Dan and Johnny getting it from one angle, and you from another. It seems as if LeGrand has *planted* those leads. It would seem that he *wants* you at the House of Pierre at this time. When you're fighting a man as clever as LeGrand, you can't afford to overlook any possibility of a trap—"

"I sincerely hope it is!" Steve Klaw cut in grimly.

Professor Gedney coughed politely to attract their attention.

"Excuse me," he said. "If I may be permitted to say something,

174

I'm almost certain, from what I have heard here, that there is some elaborate kind of trap waiting for Kerrigan, Murdoch and Klaw at the House of Pierre. From what I know of the way LeGrand operates, I would say that it seems very careless of his agents, the way they have permitted these hints about the House of Pierre to trickle out."

"Aha!" said the Chief. "So you agree with me that they shouldn't go alone? Don't you think it would be better to raid the place?"

"We haven't got a warrant, sir. And no judge would issue a warrant against such a respectable institution on the flimsy evidence we have."

"May I say just one thing more?" Professor Gedney interrupted. "Although I feel quite sure that it's a trap, I also feel that a raid will accomplish nothing. I am sure that LeGrand has facilities for covering up anything damaging, in the event of a raid in force. I believe that the only way to meet this situation is for Kerrigan, Murdoch and Klaw to go alone. In other words, for them to put themselves in the jaws of the trap!"

Steve grinned at the Chief. "What do you say, sir?"

The Chief spread his hands helplessly. "All right, Steve. You win. Go ahead. Run the thing your own way. God knows, you've earned the right. And God help you."

"Thanks for changing the Chief's mind, Professor," Klaw said gratefully.

The Professor smiled. "Now you can do me a favor in return. Take me along with you!" he begged. "I've a score of my own to settle with LeGrand. Just give me a gun, and I'll stand up right next to you!"

Gedney saw the indecision in the faces of Klaw and the Chief, and he pressed home his advantage. "Besides, I can be of material assistance. I'm familiar with the faces of many of LeGrand's agents, whom I met while I was their prisoner at the hospital. I would be in a position to warn you if I saw them—"

The Chief shrugged. "It's up to Klaw."

"Of course you can come!" Steve said heartily. "I'll get you a gun!"

CHAPTER 6
INTO THE TRAP

"I KNOW the place like a book," Professor Gedney was saying. "I've been in the House of Pierre, Ltd., a hundred times. Maurice Pierre has often invited me to examine special jewels which they have received. I find it hard to believe that Maurice is linked with Louis LeGrand!"

They were seated at a table in the Greer Restaurant, from which they had a good view of the swanky jewelry establishment across the street.

Kerrigan and Murdoch, with their informer in tow, had joined Gloria Mason, introducing themselves and setting at rest her suspicions about them. They had moved to a larger table, so that when Klaw arrived with Professor Gedney there was room for them all.

Poldi, the ex-convict informer, sat glum and sullen, saying

little. Gloria Mason was nervous. She had told them her secret, the reason why she had run out on Klaw. It was because of her father, as Steve had guessed. From something she had overheard at the hospital, she believed that her father, Obadiah Mason, was in the House of Pierre. But she didn't know whether he was there as a prisoner or as an active accomplice. She had wanted to find that out before the Suicide Squad raided the place, and that was why she had run away. If her father was really an accomplice of LeGrand, she had intended to warn him before the raid. But her courage had failed her as she had sat here in the restaurant.

But it was Poldi, the jewelry manager, who gave the show away. He looked at the electric clock.

"If you figure on doing something," he said, "you better do it quick. There isn't much time."

"Not much time?" Dan Murdoch repeated. "What do you mean?"

Poldi looked flustered. "Well, I mean—they might get away…."

The Suicide Squad exchanged glances. Johnny Kerrigan leaned forward and took a handful of Poldi's coat in his huge paw.

"Listen, punk," he growled. "We got to New York at five o'clock this morning. In one hour it'll be three o'clock. That will be ten hours after we got here, and the end of a certain deadline. Is that why you say there isn't much time?"

"No, no!" Poldi exclaimed. "I don't know what you're talking about!"

"Oh yes you do!" said Kerrigan harshly. "You were planted

there in the Crescent Department Store for us to spot, so you could tip us off to the House of Pierre. You want us to go in the House of Pierre so LeGrand can keep his promise to kill us on schedule!"

"It's a lie! I swear it's a lie!"

Kerrigan thrust him back in the chair. "We'll leave you here," he said. "If that's a trap, and we're killed, you can go and collect your reward from LeGrand. But if it's a trap and we come out of it alive, you'll get your reward all right—*from us!*"

He stood up. "Let's go, guys!"

"Just a minute," Professor Gedney stopped him. "Are you going in there without any plan?"

"That's right," Kerrigan said. "We're just going in there and let Louis LeGrand try to do his stuff. And it better be good, because it's the last chance he's going to get!"

Professor Gedney rose also. "I'm going in with you!"

"Me too!" Gloria Mason exclaimed. "If my dad's in there, I want to find him."

Kerrigan and Murdoch looked disgusted. "Sorry," said Murdoch. "The three of us are all that's going in. That's the way we work."

Stephen Klaw interrupted him. "Let them come!" he said quietly.

Dan Murdoch and Johnny Kerrigan looked at him in surprise. Those three had worked together for so long, that they were generally familiar with each other's innermost thoughts. Each of them knew that the others would never want outsiders along when they went into action. This time, they couldn't understand Steve's sudden change of mind.

But there was one thing about the Suicide Squad, which had never failed to bring them out of trouble. That thing was the unquestioning confidence that each had in the others. Among those three there was no leader, no commander. They acted almost simultaneously, as if propelled by the same instincts. But whenever any one of them saw fit to issue an order to the others, they knew that there was a crisis which demanded instant obedience. Otherwise, the one who issued the order would have taken the time to explain.

Therefore, Kerrigan and Murdoch offered no opposition.

"Thank you!" said Professor Gedney.

"JOHNNY AND Dan, you'll go in the front with Gloria," Steve said crisply. "I'll take the rear, with Professor Gedney. He knows the place; he can take me in through that back exit off the alley. When you come in the front, create a diversion there. Start a row, get their attention and keep it, so the Professor and I can work our way upstairs. There's a mezzanine in there, according to the Professor, and we'll try to get to it and hide out. If LeGrand is really set to trap us and his men see that only two of us have come, they may decide to take you two. The minute they go after you, start shooting. Gedney and I will take them in the rear from the balcony."

Kerrigan and Murdoch nodded. "You and the Professor go ahead, Shrimp. We'll give you a couple of minutes to get to the mouth of the alley, then we'll go in."

Kerrigan, Murdoch and Klaw exchanged glances, which were,

in reality, silent goodbyes. Johnny and Dan knew there was something which Steve wanted to tell them if he could, and they could only guess. They might never see him alive again. But they only grinned, nodded, and then Steve took Professor Gedney's arm and led him out of the restaurant.

They crossed the street, and Professor Gedney nodded in the direction of the traffic cop at the corner.

"If that officer only knew what a drama was being staged, under his nose, so to speak!"

Steve grunted. He glanced back when they got across, and saw that Kerrigan and Murdoch, with Gloria Mason between them, were just leaving the restaurant.

"Come on, Professor," he said. "Let's get this over with!"

Gedney smiled. "I never knew anyone in such a hurry to die!"

They walked down the side street, past the House of Pierre, Ltd., until they came to the mouth of the alley. Here, Gedney took the lead. About twenty feet down the alley there was a small entrance in the rear of the building. Gedney tried it, and found the door unlocked. He pushed it open, and stepped in, with Steve close behind him.

The transition from the bright daylight to the gloom of the interior was almost blinding for a moment. Steve thrust his hands into his pockets.

There was a short hall, at the end of which a door led out front. There was also a staircase leading up to the mezzanine.

From out front, they could hear the sound of voices raised in clamor. Steve recognized Johnny Kerrigan's booming voice among them, as well as Gloria Mason's. She was shouting, *"I want my father. What have you done with my father?"*

"Nice work," Steve whispered. "With that racket, they must have drawn off anyone who was back here!"

"This way," said Professor Gedney. He opened a door and stood to one side so Steve could go ahead.

Klaw peered into the room. It was bare, without a stick of furniture.

"What's in here?" he asked.

"The end of the road for you!" said Professor Gedney.

HE GAVE Steve a shove toward that darkened room and screamed, above the roar of the guns from within that room, *"I am Louis LeGrand! I want you to know it as you die!"*

He leaped aside, leaving Klaw to face certain death.

But Klaw wasn't quite ready for that last journey. Instead of pitching into the withering hail of fire, he twisted sideways and landed on the floor beside the doorway. The thundering barrage swept by his head, blasted into the opposite wall of the corridor.

Steve had both automatics out, and he swung them toward Gedney. But just then a group of men burst out into the hall, with their guns smoking. They had been the ones who had lain in wait there, for the signal to cut down the G-man. They came directly between Klaw and Gedney, apparently certain that they had hit their man.

Steve didn't wait. He pulled both triggers, throwing twin streams of lead into those gunmen. They went down without ever knowing what hit them.

Steve sprang to his feet, with only one shot left in each

gun. His gaze swept the corridor, but he could find no trace of Gedney.

And now another sound swept through the building—more firing, coming this time from the front of the building, where Kerrigan and Murdoch were making their stand.

The fusillade back here in the hall must have been the signal for other gunmen in the front to open up. Thus, the whole Suicide Squad was to have been cut down in one shattering, crimson moment.

Steve ran toward the front of the building. The door leading into the showroom was closed, but he did not attempt to go through that. He knew, with the instinct of a fighting man, that the attack would be coming at Kerrigan and Murdoch from the balcony above the showroom. He took those stairs two at a time, and all the while the blasting thunder of revolvers mingled with the chattering of machine-guns, told him that the other two-thirds of the Suicide Squad were still on deck.

He reached the balcony, and in a moment spotted the two machine-gunners, close to the railing, pumping shots down into the showroom. A third lay on his face sprawled across his weapon.

Lead was flying up on the balcony. Kerrigan and Murdoch were giving as good as they got. Steve couldn't figure how they had managed to remain alive down there, under that fusillade. But he didn't worry about that. He had just two shots left in his automatics, and he had to make them count.

But he had never shot a man in the back in his life, and he wasn't going to start now. He raised his right-hand automatic, took careful aim, and pulled the trigger. The slug smashed into the stock of the machine-gun wielded by the man kneeling on the right. The killer leaped up by reflex action, and a bullet from one of the guns below caught him full in the chest. He screamed, and went staggering backward with the impact.

The other machine-gunner swung around, snarling, bringing his weapon in line with Stephen Klaw—and Klaw shot him with the last remaining slug in his other automatic.

The shooting from down below ceased. Kerrigan's voice came up, mingling with the echoes of the gunfire.

"Shrimp! That sounds like you!"

Klaw grinned in the half darkness and came forward to the railing, sliding new clips into his automatics. He looked down, and saw why Kerrigan and Murdoch had been able to withstand the machine-gun fire. They had been ensconced behind the open, swinging door of the great jewelry vault down there.

"Hi, Mopes," he said.

KERRIGAN AND Murdoch came out from behind the safe door, grinning. They had Gloria Mason with them.

"Very nice work, Shrimp," said Murdoch. "Where's Gedney?"

"Disappeared," said Steve. "In case you want to know, he's really Louis LeGrand."

He left them staring up at him, and hurried down the stairs to the showroom. The building was deserted. Not a soul remained in it.

Steve joined Kerrigan and Murdoch in the showroom. "Listen, Shrimp," said Dan. "Were you wise all the time that Gedney was LeGrand?"

"I was pretty sure," Steve told him. "You see, when we found him in the ambulance, he had had the attendant tie him up, so he could ride here with it, and yet be in the clear if they should be caught. He intended to remain dead, as Professor Gedney. He was ready to bury the identity of Professor Gedney for good and all. I guess that attendant, Moe, was the only one who really knew his true identity. But Gloria, here, said that she had met him once at her father's house. Gedney made a mistake at our office. *He said he hadn't known that Obadiah Mason had a daughter!*

"Ah!" said Dan Murdoch.

"So I knew he was lying. After that, I had an open mind. Now I know. He just told me—when he thought I was headed for a one-way trip."

"He got away?" Johnny Kerrigan demanded.

Steve nodded, soberly.

"But—but—my father?" Gloria Mason said.

Steve shook his head. "I don't know, Gloria. But we'll find out yet. We're not through with Louis LeGrand—not by a long shot!"

They turned toward the front door. A crowd was staring through the shattered plate glass windows. The traffic cop from the corner was pushing his way through the crowd, and police whistles were blowing like mad.

"LeGrand has escaped through some underground passage," Dan Murdoch said softly. "He's sacrificed this whole business here—just for the sake of getting us."

"And he'll try again," said Johnny Kerrigan. "We've smashed

him in Chicago. We've smashed him in New York. But he's still in control of a powerful organization. And he hates our guts. He'll be trying again, all right, until it's finished one way or the other."

Stephen Klaw grunted. "Let's go and get a drink," he said. "We'll drink to Louis LeGrand's next try!"

POPULAR HERO PULPS AVAILABLE NOW:

THE SPIDER

- ☐ #1: The Spider Strikes $13.95
- ☐ #2: The Wheel of Death $13.95
- ☐ #3: Wings of the Black Death $13.95
- ☐ #4: City of Flaming Shadows $13.95
- ☐ #5: Empire of Doom! $13.95
- ☐ #6: Citadel of Hell $13.95
- ☐ #7: The Serpent of Destruction $13.95
- ☐ #8: The Mad Horde $13.95
- ☐ #9: Satan's Death Blast $13.95
- ☐ #10: The Corpse Cargo $13.95
- ☐ #11: Prince of the Red Looters $13.95
- ☐ #12: Reign of the Silver Terror $13.95
- ☐ #13: Builders of the Dark Empire $13.95
- ☐ #14: Death's Crimson Juggernaut $13.95
- ☐ #15: The Red Death Rain $13.95
- ☐ #16: The City Destroyer $13.95
- ☐ #17: The Pain Emperor $13.95
- ☐ #18: The Flame Master $13.95
- ☐ #19: Slaves of the Crime Master $13.95
- ☐ #20: Reign of the Death Fiddler $13.95
- ☐ #21: Hordes of the Red Butcher $13.95
- ☐ #22: Dragon Lord of the Underworld $13.95
- ☐ #23: Master of the Death-Madness $13.95
- ☐ #24: King of the Red Killers $13.95
- ☐ #25: Overlord of the Damned $13.95
- ☐ #26: Death Reign of the Vampire King $13.95
- ☐ #27: Emperor of the Yellow Death $13.95
- ☐ #28: The Mayor of Hell $13.95
- ☐ #29: Slaves of the Murder Syndicate $13.95
- ☐ #30: Green Globes of Death $13.95
- ☐ #31: The Cholera King $13.95
- ☐ #32: Slaves of the Dragon $13.95
- ☐ #33: Legions of Madness $12.95
- ☐ #34: Laboratory of the Damned $12.95
- ☐ #35: Satan's Sightless Legion $12.95
- ☐ #36: The Coming of the Terror $12.95
- ☐ #37: The Devil's Death-Dwarfs $12.95
- ☐ #38: City of Dreadful Night $12.95
- ☐ #39: Reign of the Snake Men $12.95
- ☐ #40: Dictator of the Damned $12.95
- ☐ #41: The Mill-Town Massacres $12.95
- ☐ #42: Satan's Workshop $12.95
- ☐ #43: Scourge of the Yellow Fangs $12.95
- ☐ #44: The Devil's Pawnbroker $12.95
- ☐ #45: Voyage of the Coffin Ship $12.95
- ☐ #46: The Man Who Ruled in Hell $13.95
- ☐ #47: Slaves of the Black Monarch $13.95
- ☐ #48: Machineguns Over the White House $13.95
- ☐ #49: The City That Dared Not Eat $13.95
- ☐ #50: Master of the Flaming Horde $13.95
- ☐ #51: Satan's Switchboard $13.95
- ☐ #52: Legions of the Accursed Light $13.95
- ☐ #53: The City of Lost Men $13.95
- ☐ #54: The Grey Horde Creeps $13.95
- ☐ #55: City of Whispering Death $13.95
- ☐ #56: When Thousands Slept in Hell $13.95
- ☐ #57: Satan's Shakles $14.95
- ☐ #58: The Emperor From Hell $14.95
- ☐ #59: The Devil's Candlesticks $14.95
- ☐ #60: The City That Paid to Die $14.95
- ☐ #61: The Spider at Bay $14.95
- ☐ #62: Scourge of the Black Legions $14.95
- ☐ #63: The Withering Death $14.95
- ☐ #64: Claws of the Golden Dragon $14.95
- ☐ #65: The Song of Death $14.95
- ☐ *NEW:* #66: The Silver Death Reign $14.95

THE WESTERN RAIDER

- ☐ #1: Guns of the Damned $13.95
- ☐ #2: The Hawk Rides Back from Death $13.95
- ☐ #3: Gun-Call for the Lost Legion $13.95
- ☐ #4: The Law of Silver Trent $13.95
- ☐ #5: The Gun-Prayer of Silver Trent $13.95
- ☐ #6: Silver Trent Rides Alone $13.95

G-8 AND HIS BATTLE ACES

- ☐ #1: The Bat Staffel $13.95

CAPTAIN SATAN

- ☐ #1: The Mask of the Damned $13.95
- ☐ #2: Parole for the Dead $13.95
- ☐ #3: The Dead Man Express $13.95
- ☐ #4: A Ghost Rides the Dawn $13.95
- ☐ #5: The Ambassador From Hell $13.95

DR. YEN SIN

- ☐ #1: Mystery of the Dragon's Shadow $12.95
- ☐ #2: Mystery of the Golden Skull $12.95
- ☐ #3: Mystery of the Singing Mummies $12.95

POPULAR HERO PULPS AVAILABLE NOW:

ACE G-MAN
❏ #1: The Suicide Squad Reports for Death $14.95
❏ #2: Coffins for the Suicide Squad $14.95
❏ #3: Shells for the Suicide Squad $14.95
❏ #4: The Suicide Squad in Corpse-Town $14.95
❏ *NEW:* #5: Wanted—In Three Pine Coffins $14.95

OPERATOR 5
❏ #1: The Masked Invasion $13.95
❏ #2: The Invisible Empire $13.95
❏ #3: The Yellow Scourge $13.95
❏ #4: The Melting Death $13.95
❏ #5: Cavern of the Damned $13.95
❏ #6: Master of Broken Men $13.95
❏ #7: Invasion of the Dark Legions $13.95
❏ #8: The Green Death Mists $13.95
❏ #9: Legions of Starvation $13.95
❏ #10: The Red Invader $13.95
❏ #11: The League of War-Monsters $13.95
❏ #12: The Army of the Dead $13.95
❏ #13: March of the Flame Marauders $13.95
❏ #14: Blood Reign of the Dictator $13.95
❏ #15: Invasion of the Yellow Warlords $13.95
❏ #16: Legions of the Death Master $13.95
❏ #17: Hosts of the Flaming Death $13.95
❏ #18: Invasion of the Crimson Death Cult $13.95
❏ #19: Attack of the Blizzard Men $13.95
❏ #20: Scourge of the Invisible Death $13.95
❏ #21: Raiders of the Red Death $13.95
❏ #22: War-Dogs of the Green Destroyer $13.95
❏ #23: Rockets From Hell $13.95
❏ #24: War-Masters from the Orient $13.95
❏ #25: Crime's Reign of Terror $13.95
❏ #26: Death's Ragged Army $13.95
❏ #27: Patriots' Death Battalion $13.95
❏ #28: The Bloody Forty-five Days $13.95
❏ #29: America's Plague Battalions $13.95
❏ #30: Liberty's Suicide Legions $13.95
❏ #31: Siege of the Thousand Patriots $13.95
❏ #32: Patriots' Death March $14.95
❏ #33: Revolt of the Lost Legions $14.95
❏ #34: Drums of Destruction $14.95
❏ #35: The Army Without a Country $14.95
❏ #36: The Bloody Frontiers $14.95

CAPTAIN COMBAT
❏ #1: The Sky Beast of Berlin $13.95
❏ #2: Red Wings For the Blood Battalion $13.95
❏ #3: Low Ceiling For Nazi Hell Hawks $13.95

DUSTY AYRES AND HIS BATTLE BIRDS
❏ #1: Black Lightning! $13.95
❏ #2: Crimson Doom $13.95
❏ #3: The Purple Tornado $13.95
❏ #4: The Screaming Eye $13.95
❏ #5: The Green Thunderbolt $13.95
❏ #6: The Red Destroyer $13.95
❏ #7: The White Death $13.95
❏ #8: The Black Avenger $13.95
❏ #9: The Silver Typhoon $13.95
❏ #10: The Troposphere F-S $13.95
❏ #11: The Blue Cyclone $13.95
❏ #12: The Tesla Raiders $13.95

MAVERICKS
❏ #1: Five Against the Law $12.95
❏ #2: Mesquite Manhunters $12.95
❏ #3: Bait for the Lobo Pack $12.95
❏ #4: Doc Grimson's Outlaw Posse $12.95
❏ #5: Charlie Parr's Gunsmoke Cure $12.95

THE MYSTERIOUS WU FANG
❏ #1: The Case of the Six Coffins $12.95
❏ #2: The Case of the Scarlet Feather $12.95
❏ #3: The Case of the Yellow Mask $12.95
❏ #4: The Case of the Suicide Tomb $12.95
❏ #5: The Case of the Green Death $12.95
❏ #6: The Case of the Black Lotus $12.95
❏ #7: The Case of the Hidden Scourge $12.95

THE SECRET 6
❏ #1: The Red Shadow $13.95
❏ #2: House of Walking Corpses $13.95
❏ #3: The Monster Murders $13.95
❏ #4: The Golden Alligator $13.95

CAPTAIN ZERO
❏ #1: City of Deadly Sleep $13.95
❏ #2: The Mark of Zero! $13.95
❏ #3: The Golden Murder Syndicate $13.95